ETERNAL

PATI NAGLE

Evennight Books
Cedar Crest, New Mexico

Eternal
copyright © 2012 by Pati Nagle.

ISBN: 978-1-61138-170-2

Published by Evennight Books, an imprint of Book View Café.

Cedar Crest, New Mexico.

for my sister, Carol

Acknowledgments

Thanks to Chris Krohn, Patricia Rice, and Deborah J. Ross for editing help, and to my colleagues at Book View Café for being my safety net.

I never should have let them talk me into giving blood.

Len was my best friend, but since she hooked up with Caeran I'd seen a lot less of her, which pissed me off though I tried not to let it show. Fact was, I felt like a third wheel. Now that the semester was over they were heading up north to visit his family—tonight was supposed to be our farewell fiesta after this bloodletting—and I was looking at a boring, lonely summer.

It was almost eight and the donation center was getting ready to close. Still light outside in late May, and the view of the Sandia Mountains from the picture windows was fantastic. All the couches faced those windows, for which I was thankful as I lay squeezing a little foam bar and contributing my pint.

I hated needles, and I didn't much care for the sight of blood even if it was in neat little plastic bags. I was mad at myself for letting Len wheedle me into this. Ever since she switched to pre-med, she was nuts on this kind of thing.

She and Caeran had already finished donating and were over in the lounge area with the cookies and punch. So sue me, I bleed slow.

The technician came by and jiggled my little bag of blood. "Almost done," she said cheerily.

I didn't answer. I was working up to a first class sulk.

The mountains outside were turning pink in the sunset, earning their name, "watermelon." Not as picturesque as the Sangre de Cristo mountains east of Santa Fe, named for the same reason but rather more graphically. Those Catholics.

My eye was caught by movement just outside in the

parking lot. A man, I thought, though androgynous in just the way I like: tall and slender, high cheekbones, long hair. For an instant I thought it was Caeran, but I could hear his voice behind me and he wasn't dressed like that—the stranger had on a hooded sweatshirt.

"OK, all done!"

I watched the tech remove the needle from my arm and press a patch of gauze over it. She made me hold my arm in the air for a minute, asked me if I felt dizzy, then wound some hot pink vet wrap around my elbow to secure the gauze and released me to the snacks.

I got up carefully, since I hadn't done this before. I'd heard of people passing out, but I just felt a little lightheaded, and even energized.

Len looked up and smiled as I made a beeline for the drinks. "Feeling OK?"

Ignoring her, I filled a paper cup with lemonade. It was bad, from a powdered mix. I chugged two cups.

"I'm always thirsty too," Len said. "I wish they'd have something besides all this sugar."

I glanced at Caeran, who was munching an apple. Probably he'd brought it along. He was Mr. Healthy Eater, claimed he didn't like sweets. I could have hated him if only he wasn't so damned gorgeous. And nice. Disgustingly nice.

OK, I was jealous. Len had scored the best-looking guy on campus. I'd had some dates, but none of them came close to Caeran for all-around wonderfulness. I kept telling myself I'd find the right guy eventually, but it was hard not to wish I'd spotted Caeran first. Or rather, that he'd walked up to my station at the library desk instead of Len's.

"Movie starts in twenty minutes," Len said. "We'd better go."

She and Caeran headed for the door. I hung back to look through the cookies, grabbed the last packet of Oreos and shoved a Moon Pie into my pocket, then hurried after them.

The front parking lot had been full when we arrived, so we'd parked in the lot to the north. Now the center's lot was empty except for one car at the end of the row. The pavement radiated the day's heat.

I paused to open the Oreos and stuffed one into my mouth. As I looked up, I glimpsed the guy I'd seen through the window standing by the blood red wall that surrounded the center.

His hair was long like Caeran's, but it was white even though he looked young. Goth, maybe? His clothes were black. Lean bones. I stood ogling him, then he looked at me and his nostrils flared.

I froze. Cold flooded my stomach.

He was dangerous. Not risky, *dangerous.*

I play poker. I'm used to sizing people up fast, and I trust my gut.

I looked away from him, as if that would make me invisible. Yeah, I know—acting like a frightened animal, but I had to get out of there. I started after Len and Caeran, head down, walking as fast as I could.

The cookie in my mouth was too dry to swallow. I got ready to spit and scream.

I rounded the corner of the building. A lot of the cars were gone from this lot, too. Caeran and Len were opening the doors of her Subaru.

I lost my cool and ran. When I had the car between me and the stranger, I finally had the nerve to look back.

Either he hadn't followed me, or he was invisible. I became aware that my mouth was full and started chewing.

"You OK, Manda?" Len said over the car.

I shook my head. Chewed madly and swallowed.

"There was a guy—a scary guy. In the parking lot. Looked a little like you," I said to Caeran, "except his hair was white."

Caeran and Len exchanged a wide-eyed glance, then Caeran took off running for the front of the building. I hadn't expected that.

"Get in the car," Len said.

I got in back, my usual place. Len got in the driver's side and locked the doors, then turned in her seat and looked back at me.

"Where did you see him?"

"In the parking lot. I saw him out the window earlier, too. What kind of creep hangs around the blood donor center?"

Len frowned instead of answering, then looked out the windshield. "White hair? You're sure?"

"Yeah, I'm sure."

Caeran was coming back. Len unlocked the doors and he got in.

"He was gone. He must have seen me."

Len gave him a worried look. "You can't tell...?"

"No."

They stared at each other for a long while. They do that a lot. I had always chalked it up to mushy stuff, but this was not a romantic moment.

Caeran turned to me. "I am sorry, Manda, but I think we ought to cancel the movie."

"The theater's across town. He won't bother us there, right? So, come on, let's go."

Caeran looked at Len, who showed me a smile I didn't believe. "Hey, you know how you keep bugging us to take you up to Guadalupita?" she said. "How about now?"

"Wh-hat?"

"Let's go tonight! You can come along—Madera won't mind, will he, Caeran?"

"I will call and ask."

They'd been planning to leave in the morning. Guadalupita is way the hell north of Albuquerque, a good four hours plus of driving, or so Len liked to complain. She said it was worth it, but even if we left that minute we wouldn't reach it until midnight at the earliest.

Caeran had his cell phone to his ear. I heard a buzzy sound that was the answering party.

"It's Caeran. Would you mind if we came up tonight and brought a friend?"

An inquisitive buzz. Caeran answered in another language. Might have been French—it was all smooth and flowy. Or it could have been Italian. What did I know? I suck at languages.

It wasn't Spanish, though. Spanish I could recognize. Growing up in New Mexico gives you that.

He talked a little more, then hung up and put the phone away. "Madera says that Manda is welcome."

"Great!" Len's smile looked pasted on. "Let's go pack you a bag, girlfriend!"

"Wait a minute—"

"Oh, did you have plans for the weekend?"

I glared at her. Of course I didn't, other than wallowing in some ice cream after they were gone. Maybe a poker tournament.

She smiled a real smile now. A worried smile.

"Humor me, OK, Man?"

"What are you not telling me? Other than the usual stuff you don't tell me."

"I'll explain on the road. Let's get out of town before it gets dark."

She started the car and drove to my dorm. Len used to live in the neighboring dorm, but she and Caeran were now sharing a house in the student ghetto. My loss; Len had been my best buddy on campus. We still hung out, but not as much as before.

The campus streetlights had come on, casting a warm glow on the adobe-colored stucco of the buildings. They roused a memory from months before.

"Hey, Len—you know maybe it was that guy you saw last fall that had you so freaked out. The one that might have been the campus killer? You said he had white hair, right?"

"It was not him," Caeran said flatly.

"What if it was?"

"That guy is dead," Len said.

"How do you know?"

"I just know, OK?"

I slumped back in my seat and crossed my arms. I hated it when they kept secrets from me. They did it a lot, actually. Usually I could ignore it, but my blood sugar was whacked and I was in a bad mood.

I picked up the package of Oreos, which I had dropped on the seat beside me. They were a bit crunched up, and decided I'd had enough sugar. I needed protein, like a big burger or something. With fries.

Len parked behind my dorm, and Caeran announced he wanted to stretch his legs before the drive. The words sounded casual but the way he looked around when he got out of the car was anything but. Not until he gave the nod did Len open her door.

Caeran walked us to the dorm and waited outside while Len came up to my room with me. She sat on my bed and watched me rifle my bureau for clothes to shove into my gym bag.

"Do I need anything dressy?"

"In Guadalupita?" She guffawed. "No. Bring a sweater, it gets cold up there. And bring your cell phone charger."

Odd recommendation, since ninety percent of the calls and texts I got came from her, but I tossed the charger in my bag and went to fetch my toothbrush and stuff from the bathroom I shared with my neighbor. I considered makeup, but skipped it since Len had said there was no need to be dressy. I usually only wore it on days when I worked at the library.

I came back and dumped my grooming gear into the bag. Added the book I was currently reading. Looked around trying to decide if I needed anything else.

I should have been excited. I'd wanted to visit Guadalupita ever since Len told me how beautiful it was. And I was curious to meet Madera, who was Len's mentor outside of college. He was a curandero, and I suspected he was the one who had talked her into going into pre-med, since she'd had zero interest in medicine before she'd gone with Caeran to visit him.

But the episode with the guy at the blood center threw a shadow over things. Len wasn't telling me everything, and that bugged me. I zipped up my bag and looked at her.

"How do you know the guy from last fall is dead?"

She stared at the floor. "I was there, OK?"

I gaped. "You were there? What happened?"

"I didn't see. I only saw him before, and heard about it after."

I frowned. "And?"

"And that's really all I can tell you. I'm sorry."

Hiding my annoyance, I grabbed my favorite sweater and draped it over my shoulder. "I need to hit an ATM."

"OK," Len said.

"And a McQuack's or something. Some place with fries."

"Blake's is better."

"Deal."

We went downstairs and found Caeran waiting for us in the lobby. He gave me a brief smile, and Len a long glance, then took my bag as we headed out to the car.

"We need to make a couple of stops," Len said.

Caeran nodded as he stashed my gym bag in the trunk. The first stop was their house, to get their bags. I went in with them, just because I loved their house. It was full of plants and beautiful art and stained glass and crystals in the windows. Len said the art was Caeran's. The plants must be too, because she'd never been a plant person before.

We grabbed the bags, got some cash from an ATM and then got on the freeway, stopping at a Blake's on the way out of town. I splurged on a deluxe green chile cheeseburger with fries and a chocolate malt. Len got a grilled cheese sandwich. Caeran drove while we ate.

By then the sky had darkened to the glowing blue of twilight. Venus was hanging bright in the western sky.

"So, Len." I leaned between the front seats, offering my fries. "You were going to explain why the change in plans?"

"The guy you saw is dangerous," she said, taking a fry.

Tell me about it.

"Like the guy from last fall?" I said, hoping to pry more details from her. "He was the campus killer, wasn't he?"

The killer hadn't been caught, but the killings had stopped. Right after Len had gone up to Guadalupita with Caeran, come to think of it.

Len glanced at Caeran. "Yes."

"And the guy I saw is like him?"

"Yes," Caeran said. "He is very dangerous. It was unfortunate that he saw you."

"You think he might come after me? Is that why we're leaving town? That's kind of crazy, isn't it? I mean he doesn't know who I am."

"He is a tracker," Caeran said. "He could find you if he wanted to."

"Well, I guess he won't unless he's a bloodhound."

Caeran shifted in his seat but didn't say anything. I

stuffed a couple of fries in my face, remembering the way the guy had looked at me. Yeah, I was glad to be driving away from him.

"What are these guys, some kind of cult? Or a gang?"

No answer.

Len put on some music—guitar, gentle and soothing. "So have you decided what to do this summer?"

OK, they didn't want to talk about the creepy guy. Fine.

"Not sure. Might play in some poker tournaments. Or take on more hours at the library. Benny and Vic are both leaving, you know. Summer's pretty quiet and Dave doesn't want to hire a new person."

"You're going to keep your dorm room?"

"Cheaper than an apartment."

We chatted about summer and school. Len was looking into possible jobs in the medical lab. If she did that, she'd quit the library and I'd see even less of her.

We made a pit stop in Santa Fe, then went east through the pass, then north to Las Vegas, which is a sleepy college town, nothing like its more famous counterpart in Nevada. Took another break there at a convenience store. I bought ice cream just because, then we headed on north toward Mora.

Northern New Mexico is beautiful, but it was dark so I couldn't admire the landscape. I had to content myself with staring out the window at the stars while I ate my toffee ice cream bar. Albuquerque has too much light pollution; you can only see a few stars in the city. Here the Milky Way poured across the sky in all its glory.

Somewhere along the way I fell asleep. I was muzzily aware of the car's engine shutting off, then a car door opening and closing woke me up.

I sat up, groggy. It took me a minute to remember why I was in Len's car. I heard the trunk open and then Len turned to look at me.

"Hey, you're awake!"

"Mrph."

"We're here."

Len got out and went back to the trunk. I rubbed my face, then undid my seat belt and got out.

We were parked in front of a sprawling adobe house that looked a million years old. All across the front was a shaded wooden *portal*. A light glowed by the big double doors, casting a broad pool of golden light on the wood. There was no other building in sight, just a dirt driveway and the big, open field surrounding the house.

Caeran handed me my gym bag and led the way to the door. He pulled a cord that set bells jingling somewhere back in the house.

Madera must have been waiting up for us. He came to the door right away and opened it wide into an entryway full of plants. He looked a lot like Caeran—tall and slim, chiseled face—except his hair was black instead of red-brown. He wore it loose over a caftan, and it hung to his waist. He smiled when Len introduced me.

"Welcome, Amanda," he said in a deep, quiet voice. His gazed fixed on my pink vet wrap, then he looked at Len, whose vet wrap was purple. "What is this?"

"Oh—we gave blood today." Len started picking at her vet wrap. "We could probably take these off now."

"Wait a moment," Madera said, frowning. "Come in here."

He led us through a doorway to the right and into a big, long great room with a dining table at the far end. Near the table was another door. Madera went through, leaving us alone.

I looked at Len, but before I could make a smart remark, Madera was back with a little bottle of brown glass. "This will help you heal more quickly."

We undid our wrappings and Madera rubbed a little oil on each of our punctures. It had a faintly green smell, and tingled a little while he rubbed it in. He insisted on doing Caeran's arm, too, then he corked the bottle.

"Thanks," I said.

"You are welcome. No doubt you are also tired after your journey. I have rooms ready for you."

He led us through the far door, which opened onto an interior courtyard. This really was an old-style hacienda, built for defense against marauding Indians or covetous neighbors. Surrounding an inner courtyard was a covered *portal* enclosed in glass that was obviously a modern addition. A door in each glass wall stood open to the night, which was getting chilly. Len was right, it was cold up here even in early summer. I wished I'd put on my sweater.

As Madera led us along the *portal* I admired the courtyard through the glass. *Plazuela,* my brain supplied at random. Thank you, New Mexico history class.

The *plazuela* was paved in flagstone and had patio furniture and bushes scattered around. I smelled lilacs and heard the trickle of water. I spotted the fountain at the west side just before Madera opened a door on the right and went in. A moment later the room filled with soft light, and he came back to the door, gesturing welcome.

"This room is for you, Amanda. The bathroom is next door."

Cozy. Bed, nightstand, dresser, all of rustic pine carved in a vaguely Spanish style. A decanter and water glass stood on the dresser. The warm light was coming from from a lamp on the nightstand. There was even a kiva fireplace.

"It's beautiful. Thanks so much."

I was too tired to be more eloquent. Madera said goodnight and led Len and Caeran away along the *portal.* I watched them turn the corner and then closed the door.

So tired. And confused about the creepy guy. Sure, I never wanted to see him again. The solution was simple: stay away from the blood donor center. No problem.

Except my gut had told me in no uncertain terms to flee. And Caeran had said he was a tracker.

I wondered how Caeran knew, but there was no use worrying about it. We were far from Albuquerque now. Might as well enjoy the weekend.

I plugged in my cell phone, then dug out my toothbrush and headed for the bathroom. As I came out of my door I thought I saw movement to my left, but by the time I looked there was nothing. Frowning, I walked all the way to the door into the living room at end of the passage.

I stood listening but all I heard was the fountain and a cricket chirping somewhere. Finally I gave up, went back and found the bathroom, brushed teeth, washed face, then returned to my room to hit the sack.

There was an old-fashioned hook latch on the door. It wouldn't hold up to a good kick, but I latched it anyway, and felt better.

I got in bed and lay listening to the nothing. It's really quiet in the country—you don't realize how noisy the city is until you get away from all the traffic and airport rumble. The silence of rural areas bothers some city people, but I love it. Whether it was the peacefulness or the fact that I'd given blood, I fell asleep immediately.

~

I woke up thinking I was at Grandma's, because I smelled fresh baked bread. Sat up, figured out where I was, and hopped into my clothes. The little poke on my arm was almost completely gone—I had to look hard to see it, and it was just slightly tender. I dragged a brush through my hair and went out to find the bread.

When I opened my door, I gasped. The *plazuela* was filled with color: lilacs, both purple and white, coppery and yellow wild roses, iris in a rainbow of colors. I walked out through the nearest door in the glass wall and stood taking it all in. Floral fragrances blended with the baking smells. I wanted to eat all of it.

Promising myself I'd spend some time out here reading, I followed my nose across the *plazuela* and into the *portal* on the far side. I heard voices from down the passage. Continuing that direction, I found an open door into the kitchen.

Four men were sitting at a table by a window that overlooked the *plazuela*. They were all heavy on the Caeran DNA—same hair color, same green eyes. They were talking in the fluid language I'd heard Caeran use on the phone, but when I came in they clammed up and sat staring at me.

My heart did a little joyful skip. Four Caeran clones! Maybe one of them was unattached. I gave them a hesitant smile.

Madera was standing by the stove. He looked up at me and smiled.

"Good morning, Amanda. Please come in."

He gestured toward a Mexican tile counter where there was half a loaf of bread, butter and jam, a bowl of sliced strawberries, and a teapot under a cozy. I went straight for the bread, which was still warm. It steamed a little when I whacked off a big slice, and the butter melted into it. I took a bite and my mouth exploded in bliss.

The conversation started up again behind me, in quieter tones. Self-conscious, I stayed by the counter and poured myself a cup of tea.

Madera was watching me. I swallowed the last of my bread. "This is wonderful. Thank you." I glanced toward the table and added in a whisper, "I didn't know you had other guests."

"These are my neighbors. Would you like to meet them?"

Boy, howdy—except that I felt strangely shy. I took another swallow of tea and nodded.

Madera went over to the table and I followed a step behind him. The guys there stopped talking and looked up at us.

"I would like to introduce Amanda," Madera said. "She is my guest for a while. Amanda, these are Faranin, Lomen, Bironan, and Nathrin."

Wow, wild names. I would never remember them all.

I smiled. "Hi."

Three of them just gave me serious nods. The fourth one, Nathrin, actually smiled.

"I am glad to meet you. You are a friend of Lenore?"

"Um, yeah."

"She is a good soul."

I didn't know what to say to that, so I just nodded. He was nice, I decided. His face was a little longer than Caeran's, but in the dark I couldn't have told them apart.

As if summoned by my thoughts, Caeran walked in. He had Len's car keys in his hand.

"Good morning, Manda. Did you sleep well?"

"Like a dead thing."

He looked confused, then smiled and turned to his four doppelgangers. "Are you ready?"

They got up from the table and collected backpacks from a *banco* by the fireplace at the far end of the room. I looked at Caeran.

"Going somewhere?"

"My cousins need a ride to Albuquerque. I'll be back tomorrow."

Five guys squished into Len's car for that long a drive? Must be something important.

Caeran exchanged a few words of flowy-talk with Madera, then led the other four away. I watched, kind of disappointed that I hadn't gotten to talk with them more.

I looked toward the stove. Madera was watching me as he stirred a pot.

"Thanks for the welcome," I said. "It's really nice of you, especially since you weren't expecting me."

"As you can see, I have plenty of room."

"Well, if I can help with anything—"

"Is there any tea left? Hi, Manda," said Len as she came in carrying a mug. She took the cozy off the teapot and lifted the lid. "I'm going to kill it. Should we make more?"

"Yes, please," Madera said. "Amanda, would you fill this kettle?"

"Sure."

While I was at the sink, Madera opened a pottery jar and scooped out some black leaves, putting them into a little strainer thingie. I was impressed—I'd only ever used teabags. He set the strainer aside, took the kettle from me and put it on the stove, then washed out the teapot and put the strainer into it.

I felt like I was in the way, so I cut another slice of bread and slathered it with butter, put some berries in a bowl as a gesture toward healthy eating, and went over to the table where Caeran's cousins had been sitting. Len joined me, bringing both our mugs.

"Thanks. Caeran has a big family, eh?"

Len sipped her tea. "Yes and no."

She didn't elaborate, and I wasn't going to rise to the bait and ask. "Nice of him to drive them to Albuquerque. Hope he brings your car back with a full tank."

"He will."

Of course he would. He was Mr. Wonderful.

I stifled a sigh and watched Madera, who was back at the

stove, looking graceful as he stirred his pot. His hair was braided today. His profile made me think of the beautiful people in Maxfield Parrish paintings. I had expected Len's mentor to be older.

He didn't really look Spanish—not like most of the locals. He was too tall, too pale. Aristocratic, with that aquiline nose. Maybe Old World Spanish looked like that, but most New Mexican Hispanics had a lot of New World blood mixed in.

Well, he had some Caeran blood, or something close to it. Not as striking a match as the cousins, but clearly the same family.

My thoughts drifted off to my own family back in Portales. My parents were very straight, very conservative, and they'd raised me and my brother strictly. He'd been a super-jock in school and got drafted into a minor league baseball team before graduation. I'd rebelled in high school and escaped to UNM and Albuquerque as soon as possible.

Sometimes I missed home, but whenever I went back to visit I remembered why I'd left. I loved my parents—especially at a distance.

I finished my berries and decided I'd better get away from the bread, so I filled my mug with milk and headed for the *plazuela*. The morning was pleasantly cool. In Albuquerque things were already summer-hot.

I sat in a chair in the shade and watched a swarm of birds playing in the fountain. The smell of lilacs made me relax. Yeah, I could get used to this.

A wild thought of giving up my dorm room and spending the summer here occurred to me, but I squashed it. For one thing, I had a job. For another, it would be a serious imposition, unless I could make it up to Madera somehow. No, I should forget that.

I had the weekend, since I assumed Len and Caeran would drive me home on Sunday. I told myself I was damn lucky for that.

I heard the kettle whistle in the kitchen and was glad, because it was almost too chilly outside. I finished my milk, then headed for my room to get my book. On the way I decided to make a pit stop at the bathroom. Just as I reached the door it was opened by yet another Caeran clone.

"Oh, sorry!"

I stepped back, taking him in. His hair was a little darker than Caeran's and his eyes were a softer green. I smiled.

"You must be another guest of Madera's. Or a neighbor?"

"Guest," he said in a quiet voice. His eyes were troubled and he looked tired. I didn't remember ever seeing Caeran look tired.

"I'm Amanda Richards. I'm here with Len and Caeran."

"Len is here?"

I nodded. "She's in the kitchen, or she was."

He glanced toward the kitchen and nodded absently. Didn't offer his name.

Awkward moment of the day number one. He was between me and the bathroom, I was between him and the door to the *plazuela*. His gaze had fixed on something—or maybe nothing—out in the garden.

I cleared my throat. "Well, nice meeting you."

He looked at me in faint surprise. I answered with a smile and glanced toward the bathroom. He seemed to figure it out finally and took a step backward, then turned and headed away down the *portal*. He went into the last door before the living room.

I had to find a better way of talking to these guys. I mean, I had now met, what, five gorgeous men? And not managed to make one of them take an interest in me.

Well, we'd see about that. I just hadn't gotten a read on them, that was all. They were different—maybe foreign. Caeran had mentioned Europe a couple of times, come to think of it.

I smiled to myself. I liked a challenge. Len had her dream guy, why couldn't I have one too?

= 2 =

I got my book and went back outside. My mug was now full of steaming tea. I glanced up toward the kitchen with a smile and said, "Thanks," as if anyone could hear me. Maybe Madera could see me through the window.

He was a great host. I'd have to write him a thank you note after I went home.

I settled back into my chair in the garden, wondering idly if I should try for Madera. Or maybe the friendly one. The other three I'd met that morning were standoffish, and the guy I'd just bumped into was preoccupied.

Len came out and joined me; she'd found a book somewhere. We both sat there reading until the shade receded, then we moved into the *portal* where there were more chairs, and sat reading until Madera called us into the kitchen for lunch.

He'd made a wonderful soup with chicken and potatoes and green chile. More of the fresh bread on the side, and iced tea. We sat at the table by the window and Len drove the conversation, telling me things about Madera that I could ask questions about.

"Know what? Madera made all the carved furniture in the house himself."

He shot a glance at Len. "Not all. Some pieces are from clients."

"Healing clients?" I said. "You take payment in trade?"

"That is all that many of them can afford."

I nodded. Rural parts of New Mexico were painfully poor. Portales had ENMU, so it had a stable source of employment, but it was also huge compared to Guadalupita.

Or so I believed. I hadn't actually seen Guadalupita on the way in, but Len always said it was nothing but a bar and a post office and a couple of houses, and that if it weren't for Caeran's cousins, Madera would be lonely.

That reminded me of the mystery clone I had met. I checked the table—no fourth place setting.

"Is your other guest not coming to lunch?"

Len looked up. "Other guest?"

"Savhoran," said Madera. He looked at me. "I gather you've met him."

"Briefly. He didn't actually tell me his name."

"I took him some soup earlier. He is a patient as well as a guest, and spends most of his time in his room."

"Still?" Len asked softly.

Madera nodded, and looked down at his bowl. I wanted to ask what was wrong with Savhoran, but I chickened out.

"This soup is great," I said instead.

"Thank you."

We talked about unimportant things for the rest of the meal. I learned a lot about Madera's numerous talents, and about how he lived out here in the country. He grew some of his own food, and most of the rest came in trade for healing. He had an extensive herb garden—I made admiring noises and was promised a tour—an orchard, a vineyard, and chickens and goats. I wondered how much land he owned, but that was another nosy question I kept to myself. Despite his friendliness, he came across as a very private person.

After lunch I went back to reading on the *portal* while Madera took Len off to consult on something or other. He was her mentor; that's what she was here for. Interesting how she was blending modern medicine with folk medicine. I wondered what her profs thought of it.

The sun shifted to the west, so I moved to the north side

of the *portal*, near my room. There were chairs here too—there were chairs scattered all the way around the *portal*. Madera could have thrown a pretty big party if he'd wanted.

I kept going back to the kitchen for more iced tea until I finished off the pitcher. Finished my book late in the afternoon. Still no sign of Len. I put my feet up on a hassock and closed my eyes.

I must have dozed off, because when I heard a door closing I looked up and it was late. The sun had set, and the *plazuela* glowed with soft evening light. I got up and stretched, then noticed fantastic smells on the air. I couldn't identify them other than that it was dinner and it made my mouth water.

I picked up my empty glass to take back to the kitchen, then noticed I wasn't alone. Sav—Sav—that Sav guy was standing near the corner, looking out at the garden.

He noticed me. I smiled and gave a little wave.

"Hi."

Wasn't sure what else to say. Awkward to ask if he was feeling better.

Come on, Man. Try harder.

I walked over to him. "You're one of Caeran's cousins, right?"

He nodded.

"Have you lived in New Mexico long?"

"No."

Right. OK, if he wasn't going to help, I wouldn't pester him.

I almost left right then, but I had this feeling he must be lonely. For sure he was sad. I decided to stay a little longer.

He was looking at the garden again. The birds were gone now, and the fountain's trickle was peaceful.

"Beautiful place," I said.

"Yes."

He nodded, then looked straight at me for the first time. My breath caught in my throat—just like it had when the creep at the blood center had looked at me—but this was a *good* feeling. He *saw* me.

"I am Savhoran."

I smiled. "Amanda. Nice to meet you."

His manner was kind of formal, but I figured it was just shyness. With almost painful politeness, he asked, "Have *you* been in New Mexico long?"

"Born and raised. I'm from Portales."

He nodded. I would have bet money he had no clue where Portales was.

"It's south and east," I added. "Out on the plains. Windy and hot. This is much nicer—Madera's really created an oasis here."

Savhoran smiled, but still looked sad. I wanted to ask him what was wrong, maybe try to comfort him, but I didn't. Too nosy on such short acquaintance, and it was obviously some health problem since he was here as a patient.

"Well, dinner smells great," I said. "Are you headed for the kitchen?"

He hesitated. I didn't give him a chance to say "no."

"Come on."

I nodded toward the *plazuela*, and stuck my hand out without thinking. He didn't take it, but he did come with me.

The flagstones were warm with the heat of the day. Savhoran stopped in the middle of the *plazuela*, looking at the flowers and the fountain as if he'd never seen anything so beautiful. I watched him cup a spray of lilacs in his hand and smell it. The creases in his forehead relaxed.

We went to the kitchen and found Len and Madera busy with supper. The room was lit with the soft glow of oil lamps on the counters and in a chandelier. Candles were burning in a pottery wrath on the table, which was set for three.

Madera looked up from carving a roasted chicken and smiled with delight. "Good evening," was all he said.

Len glanced at Savhoran as she finished putting rice into a serving bowl. "Hi, there, stranger!"

He acknowledged the tease with a half smile. Len told us to sit down, we were in the way, then she quietly set a fourth place.

I made a halfhearted offer to help, but everything was almost ready. Len brought bowls of rice and spinach to the table, and Madera brought over a platter of sliced chicken. That was what smelled so wonderful.

"Boy, Caeran will be sorry he missed this," I said. "I thought he'd be back by now."

Len and Madera traded a glance.

"He called," Len said. "He's got some things he wants to do in town, so he's staying over."

Trouble in paradise? She didn't look distressed, but she didn't look jolly either. It was none of my business, so I kept quiet.

There was wine—red, in an unlabeled bottle. Madera poured and everyone helped themselves to the food. Savhoran took tiny portions, but I didn't. I was starving even though I'd hardly moved all afternoon.

"I hope you enjoyed the day," Madera said to me.

I nodded and took a sip of wine. "It was nice—this is good!—nice to just relax."

"If you need more to read, I have a small library. Not many current titles, I fear, but you are welcome to look at them."

"Thanks."

I took a bite of the chicken and almost moaned aloud. It was fall-apart tender, with pepper and garlic and a tang of lemon. Heavenly.

Len and Madera chatted about his garden while we ate.

He was just now putting out tomatoes and cucumbers, because it froze late into May this far north. I gathered that he had a greenhouse somewhere.

I admired people who grew their own food. I'd tried, but the climate in Portales is pretty unforgiving and only determined gardeners can get stuff to grow there.

"I'd love to help if there's anything I can do," I said. "I'm not much of a gardener, but I can pull weeds."

"I will take you up on that tomorrow."

"Great!"

I meant it. If I made myself useful, maybe I'd get invited back.

Madera was watching Savhoran push rice around his plate. He'd eaten some of the spinach, but the tiny slice of chicken was untouched. He sensed Madera's gaze and looked up, and said something in that flowy language.

"It's all right," Madera said softly. "I can heat up some broth if you like."

Savhoran shook his head and stared unhappily at his food.

It sucks being sick, and it's sad to watch a beautiful creature suffer. I felt sorry for him and wished there was something I could do. Best thing I could think of was not to make an issue of it, so I pretended it wasn't important and finished my own supper.

Savhoran left as soon as we were done. I stayed to help with the dishes, figuring he probably wasn't in the mood for company. Madera didn't have a dishwasher, so Len washed and I dried while our host put away the leftovers.

"I still think you should get a hot tub," Len said over her shoulder.

"It would use too much electricity," said Madera.

"Not if you got one of those soft ones. They're really efficient."

"I much prefer hot springs."

"Yeah, but it's a mile hike to the closest one! And no bathroom, no shower—"

"Conveniences, but not necessary. Shall we go into the living room?"

Len handed me the last plate to dry. "You're changing the subject."

"Yes." He smiled. "Will you play the guitar?"

She sighed and took the towel from me, drying her hands. "OK, you win."

Madera's gaze shifted to me. "Unless you don't like music."

"Oh, I love it. I just wish I had talent like Len."

"We each have our own gifts."

He led the way into the living room, lit some oil lamps in *nichos* in the wall, then laid a fire in the kiva fireplace in one corner of the room. Len fetched a guitar case from behind a bookcase, took out the guitar and started tuning it. I sat on a *banco* and watched Madera build the fire.

He didn't use any paper, just some smaller sticks as kindling. Must be a traditionalist on fire-building, like he was on other things. He did have electricity and gas or propane for the stove, but he didn't have a lot of appliances, and he seemed to prefer firelight to electrical.

Len started to strum the guitar and I looked at her, trying to recognize the music. A flare of light from the fireplace made me glance back. Whatever Madera had used, it worked a treat. The fire settled into a cheerful crackle.

Len played some folk songs and I chimed in on the chorus of the ones I knew. My voice isn't polished like hers, but I can carry a tune. I even filled in a harmony here and there.

She mixed in some more current songs and some old 70's stuff—James Taylor and some of the Beatles' mellower songs.

Gentle music. Relaxing and peaceful.

She was just winding up "You've Got A Friend" when I glanced toward the dining table and saw Savhoran standing there. He must have come in by the far door. I smiled and gestured for him to join us. He hesitated, then came over and sat on the *banco* on the other side of the fireplace.

Len sang a couple more songs, then handed the guitar to Madera. He played some flamenco-sounding music, then to my surprise began to sing in Spanish.

His voice was even more rich singing than speaking. I watched him, entranced, trying to catch the meaning of the words, though I only recognized a few. The song had a lamenting tone, and I found myself glancing at Savhoran.

He was leaning against the fireplace, eyes closed. I couldn't help staring at him. So beautiful, so sad. How could I make him feel better?

He opened his eyes. For a second I felt like he'd heard my thoughts, but he didn't look at me. He stared at the floor, then looked up at Madera, who gave the guitar back to Len and went to join Savhoran on the *banco*.

They talked too quietly for me to hear, maybe in their language. Len played some soft chords, then launched into a Norah Jones song I didn't know the words to. I listened, feeling disappointed and not knowing why.

Madera said something to which Savhoran nodded, then got up and left the room. Len watched Madera go with a raised eyebrow, but kept singing. Savhoran listened to her for a while, then his gaze drifted to me.

Oh, man. When he looked at me I felt like a spotlighted deer—in a good way, if that makes any sense. I wanted to do whatever it would take to make him smile.

He smiled.

Weird. Could he really tell what I was thinking?

Len finished the song, and because I felt embarrassed I

applauded. Savhoran did, too.

"Your music is beautiful," he said.

"Oh, thanks," Len said, flashing a self-conscious smile. "Not my music, actually. I mean I didn't write it."

"You play it beautifully."

"Thanks." She looked at me. "What next? I'm out of ideas."

I said the first thing I could think of. "'Across the Sea.'"

She'd learned to play it when *Lord of the Rings* came out. When we'd met we discovered we both loved the movies, and we sang that song obsessively for about six months our first year at school. It was burned into my brain.

Savhoran listened, watching me as much as he watched Len. I tried to pretend I didn't notice, but I had goosebumps by the end of the song.

Len went on to play her other favorites from the movies; "May It Be" and a couple of the songs in elvish, which I'd never bothered to learn. Savhoran listened with an amused expression, and applauded politely.

Madera came back with a tray of tea, cups, and a bowl of tiny strawberries. I was yearning for coffee, but this would have to do. Madera must not be a coffee person. I hadn't seen a coffeemaker in the kitchen.

I didn't need coffee this late anyway, I told myself, and thanked Madera for the cup he handed me. The tea was light and flowery. I took a couple of the berries and marveled at their sweetness.

Savhoran ate one strawberry, spent a lot of time chewing it, and washed it down with the rest of his tea. Madera refilled his cup without commenting. I held my cup out too, and ate some more of the berries, pretending I hadn't noticed Savhoran's trouble.

"How long have you lived here?" I asked Madera.

"Oh, decades."

He didn't look old enough for that, but I let it pass. "But you're not from here, right?"

He set down the teapot. "Not originally."

I turned my cup in my hands, waiting for it to cool a little. "Spain?"

"I've lived in a number of countries."

"Sorry, I didn't mean to be nosy."

"The truth is, this has been my home long enough that I don't think about the other places."

Fair enough. I sipped my tea.

It was awkward without the music. I wanted to ask all kinds of questions that were probably rude. I looked at Savhoran, saw him watching me, and gave a nervous smile. He smiled back.

Len's cell phone went off. She stood up, digging it out of her pocket, and glanced at the display.

"It's Caeran. Excuse me."

She went out into the entryway. I could hear her voice, muffled, asking questions. Left alone with two gorgeous men, I couldn't think of anything to say. Dammit.

Madera picked up the guitar and strummed it. I relaxed a little; music was an excuse for not talking. I sipped my tea and tried to think of something intelligent to say the next time there was a lull.

Len came back, looking unhappy. Madera stopped playing and turned expectantly to her. She met his gaze and shook her head.

"It's taking longer than he thought."

I frowned. Caeran had planned to be here, not in Albuquerque. This was more than just a trip to the warehouse store, I suspected. Was it the other four guys causing the delay?

Now there was something I could talk about. Grasping at straws, I tried to remember any of the Caeran-clones' names.

Nathan? Nathrin!

I looked at Madera. "So those other guys—Nathrin and them—you said they're your neighbors?"

He nodded. "They are building a house nearby."

That only led to more questions I shouldn't ask—were they building on Madera's land? What had they needed so much that they could only get it in Albuquerque, and why it had taken all four of them to go after it?

"Have you known them long?"

"Not long at all. I met them last fall."

I looked at Len. Last fall was when Caeran had first brought her up here. Had he not known Madera, then? But they all looked so alike...

I was thinking too hard. I stood up, leaving my mug on the table.

"Think I need some air. Please excuse me."

I went out through the entryway and a glass door into the *portal* around the *plazuela*. It was chilly but I needed to get away and sort out my thoughts.

Savhoran was ill and I shouldn't ask nosy questions about it. I found him attractive. Neither of those things should destroy my world.

Len had secrets, but that was nothing new. Madera was in on them. I was a little jealous of that, but I could live with it.

What was Caeran up to?

It really wasn't any of my business. None of it was. Why did that upset me?

I walked out into the *plazuela* and looked up at the stars. The smell of lilacs surrounded me. The fountain murmured peacefully.

Truth was, I was an outsider. I didn't belong here. Len had a reason to be here, but I was just excess baggage. Madera was being very nice—he was the greatest host—but he probably secretly wished I was back in Albuquerque.

I sat in a lounge chair and stared up at the sky. The moon was up, really bright out here in the country. It washed out a lot of the stars. I picked out the big dipper and was proud of myself.

I heard a door close. Maybe the others had decided to turn in. I stayed where I was.

I didn't know what I wanted, that was the problem. In the grander scheme of things I had no direction.

I'd taken the job at the university library because Len worked there. She was the one who was really into books and history. I liked books, but I liked movies more. Too bad you couldn't get paid to watch movies. Or play poker—I liked that a lot, but it kind of sucked for career potential. I'd kept track of my winnings and losses since I came to Albuquerque, and I was just slightly short of breaking even.

"Hello."

I nearly jumped out of my skin. Looked up at Savhoran standing next to my chair.

"God, you scared me! Make some noise next time!"

"I am sorry—should I go?"

"No! No, it's fine. I was just startled, that's all."

He pulled a chair closer to mine and sat in it. His face was troubled, but still beautiful.

"Have the others gone to bed?" I asked.

Savhoran shook his head. "They are discussing a new treatment for me."

"Oh. I'm sorry you're not well."

He looked up at me. "Thank you."

"Wish I could help."

"You do help. You do not view me as...damaged."

"Well, you don't look damaged."

He laced his fingers between his knees and frowned at them. "My kindred believe that I am."

"What do they know?"

He laughed, but the smile faded right away. "I should have healed by now."

This was really bothering him. I sat up and turned toward him. Maybe he didn't want to talk about it, but in case he did I was listening.

He lifted his head and met my gaze. "I was injured last fall. I was attacked. The wound has healed, mostly, but... there is some chance of infection."

Oh, man. Poor guy.

"Do not worry. There is no danger to—I mean, it is not something you can catch from me."

"I wasn't worried about that."

He smiled, but still looked sad. I reached out and touched his hand, something I never would have done if I'd stopped to think about it. He froze, then his hand turned to clasp mine.

My heart started pounding. His eyes locked onto mine; I couldn't have looked away if I'd wanted to.

"You are the only one who cares for me."

"That's not true..."

"Len and Madóran are friends. That is different."

I blinked, confused. He took my other hand in his.

"My kin are uncomfortable with my infirmity. I do not blame them, but I...used to be welcome among them, and now I am not."

"That's pretty unfair."

"They have good reason. I do not blame them."

"You can't help being sick."

He smiled softly. "No. Nor can I help being lonely. I am used to being surrounded by family. Now I have no one."

I looked down, feeling the blush crawl up my neck before I even asked. "You don't have a sweetheart?"

"She has left. She could not bear to watch...my illness."

I swallowed. "Well, maybe when you're better..."

He shook his head. "She will not return. We said our farewells."

I tried really hard not to be glad about that.

Savhoran squeezed my hands and leaned forward to whisper in my ear. "Thank you for not being afraid."

His hair was tickling my cheek, and he smelled wonderful. "I could never be afraid of you," I said in a shaky whisper.

He laughed softly, his breath warm on my neck. A shiver of delight went through me. He put his cheek against mine.

Oh, man. Oh, yes.

I pulled my hands free and wrapped my arms around him. He hugged me back. We sat that way for a long time, just holding each other. It felt wonderful.

I heard a small sound and opened my eyes. Madera was standing in the front doorway, watching us.

"Savhoran," he said softly.

We separated, and while I blushed so hot I thought I'd perspire, Savhoran glanced at our host, then turned back to me. He squeezed my hands, dropped a kiss on my forehead, and left.

Damn. Damn, damn.

Through the glass walls I saw Madera lead him along the *portal* to his room. They went in and closed the door. Consultation, or maybe treatment. I wasn't invited.

Damn, damn, damn.

I sat there reliving the last few minutes for a while, then I got up and went looking for Len. She must have been helping Madera, because she wasn't in the kitchen or the living room or her room. I chickened out on searching the whole place.

Nothing else to do. I went to bed, and did some more reliving and some elaboration on the theme. I was used to fantasizing myself to sleep, but I usually didn't have this much fresh material to draw on. I didn't drift off until after the wedding.

I actually woke up early. Lying cozy in bed, I gradually remembered the previous night.

God!

I sat up. Thought about pulling on yesterday's clothes, but instead did the civilized thing and dressed in fresh everything and brushed my hair. Headed to the bathroom hoping I might run into Savhoran again, but no such luck. With teeth freshly scrubbed, I went to the kitchen which was again wreathed in tantalizing bread-baking smells, and warmth from the oven and the kiva fireplace.

The only one there was Madera. He smiled, offered me tea, and invited me to take over slicing up oranges. Hiding disappointment, I did as he asked while he went to collect some eggs.

Fresh eggs for breakfast. Seriously fresh. This guy was amazing.

Why had I ended up hugging Savhoran instead of Madera? Possibly because Madera had shown zero interest in me. He was friendly, yes, but he didn't need anything from me.

Savhoran, on the other hand, was lonely. He'd said it himself.

Damaged. He'd said that too. That ought to make me cautious, but I wasn't feeling cautious.

I stopped slicing and drifted into a daydream about the previous evening. Just imagining the feel of his arms around me gave me goosebumps.

The sound of footsteps out in the *portal* made me pick up the knife again. My heart was pounding even though I told myself it was probably Madera, or maybe Len.

"Amanda."

Savhoran's voice. I closed my eyes and smiled, then turned.

"Morning," I said, trying to keep it to a grin.

He came and stood beside me while I reached for the last orange. Just having him near made my arms tingle.

"I am sorry I had to leave last night."

ME TOO!

"There's always tomorrow," I said, trying to sound light.

"Or tonight."

My hand slipped and the knife nicked my finger. "Shit! Oh, I'm sorry. I mean 'Darn!'"

Savhoran stepped back, eyes wide as he stared at the blood welling on my finger. I bit back another curse.

Way to gross out your potential boyfriend, Man.

There were no paper towels on the counter, and I didn't want to bleed on one of Madera's nice napkins, so I brought my finger to my mouth.

"It's just a scratch."

Savhoran was staring like I'd cut off my hand. A swallow moved his throat, then his gaze met mine.

And he ran.

= 3 =

I followed him to the *portal*, sucking on my finger. I would have gone after him but Madera came in from the other direction with a small basket of eggs. Savhoran's door slammed.

Madera turned to me. "What happened?"

"I cut my finger and he freaked out."

He looked like I'd told him his mother had died, then shoved the basket into my hand and went after Savhoran. I stood frozen, watching until he disappeared into Savhoran's room.

Great, just great. Let's see how else we can screw up, shall we?

I went back to the kitchen and stuck my finger under the faucet. I was still bleeding. Some people keep their knives really sharp, which is a hazard to those of us who don't.

My stomach was in knots. I looked at the oranges and nearly cried. I'd been hungry earlier, but now the thought of food made me sick.

Len came striding into the kitchen, band-aid in hand, smiling but with worried eyes. "Here, let's put this on it."

I shut off the water and let her bandage my finger, wondering how she'd known I'd been clumsy enough to cut myself. Maybe Madera told her. She dried my hand with a wad of tissues from her pocket, put the band-aid on me, then threw the tissues onto the fire.

"Sit down, I'll fix breakfast."

I sat at the table and stared out the window in the direction of Savhoran's room. Len brought me a mug of tea from the pot that Madera had made earlier. She checked the oven, took out a loaf of bread and set it on the counter, and continued puttering. I stopped paying attention.

What had happened? It was just a little cut. Why had Savhoran reacted like that?

I had this horrible guilty feeling that I'd done something awful. I couldn't figure out why.

"I talked to Caeran," Len said over her shoulder. "He's on his way up to pick us up, so after breakfast we'd better pack."

I wanted to protest, but I couldn't figure out what to say. I was numb with disbelief.

This was surreal. Everything Len was doing was perfectly normal, expect I didn't understand why she was doing it.

She brought two plates of scrambled eggs to the table and set one in front of me, then brought over the bread on a bread board, cut off a heel, and buttered it.

"Come on, Man. Eat."

I took a forkful of the eggs and managed to chew and swallow it. All in slow motion.

Madera came in and gave Len a long look, then poured himself some tea and joined us at the table. I watched him butter a slice of bread like nothing had happened.

"Where's Savhoran?"

Madera looked up at me. "He is resting."

"What did I d-do?"

"You didn't do anything, Amanda. He is ill."

"What, he can't stand the sight of blood?"

"No." Madera's face was grim. "He can't."

Oh, jeez.

"I'm sorry. It was an accident. Will you tell him I'm sorry?"

"He knows. This isn't your fault, Amanda."

"Can I see him?"

"Not now."

I sucked a ragged breath, determined not to cry. Madera put down his bread and took my hand, wrapping his palm around my cut finger. His hand was hot. It felt good. I closed my eyes, struggling to keep it together. After a while he let me go.

I opened my eyes and saw Madera eating his breakfast. I couldn't bear to eat any more but I held my mug in both hands and sipped at the tea. I felt like I'd committed a crime and been condemned for it.

Len and Madera ate in silence. Finally Len got up, put her plate in the sink and came back for mine.

"You finished?"

I nodded. She took my plate away, scraped the uneaten food into the trash, and rinsed the plate in the sink.

"OK, let's go pack."

I wanted to ask what the hurry was—Caeran probably wouldn't arrive for hours—but I didn't trust myself to speak. We went around the *portal* to my room, passing Savhoran's door which was shut.

Len bullied me in to packing my bag, then went off to do hers. I wandered out into the *plazuela* and watched the birds squabbling in the fountain. Sat on the chair I'd been on last night, trying to make sense of it all.

My fault for getting infatuated with a wounded duck? Savhoran looked fine, but what did I know? He'd had trouble eating dinner. Apparently he was sicker than I'd thought.

Except he'd said he'd been injured. Wounded.

I leaned back in my chair, frustrated. I didn't have enough information. This must be where Len had picked up the habit of being cagey. Come to think of it, she hadn't done that before she met Caeran.

"Amanda?"

I looked up at Madera, who was standing a few feet

away. He had changed clothes, swapping his usual caftan for cotton pants and a loose cotton shirt. He had a pair of work gloves in his hand.

"Are you still willing to help me in the garden?"

I stared at him for a minute. Gardening? I thought I was being sent home.

I sighed and got up. "Sure."

He handed me the gloves and led me through the south side of the house, out into a huge, gorgeous garden. It was bigger than the whole back yard of the house I'd grown up in, laid out in a patchwork instead of rows; squares of different kinds of plants.

Madera held out a straw hat he'd picked up on the way through the house. I put it on and followed him between patches of leafy stuff, down to an area where nothing was growing. There were several small mounds of dirt, maybe a foot and a half across, in a square pattern. A tray of baby plants in pots sat nearby.

"If you would dig places for these, like this..."

He took up a trowel and crouched by one of the mounds, carefully making a hole in its center. Then he handed the trowel to me and went to get one of the plants. I watched him set it in the hole and gently press dirt around it. He looked up at me and I nodded.

The sun was warm, baking the earth and raising the smell of summer. I bent to the work, thinking he was just humoring me, getting me out of the house so I wouldn't bother Savhoran. I bit my lip, determined to stay cool.

Madera went and got a hose that he used to water the plant he'd just put in the ground, then brought two more pots from the tray and went to work on the holes I had made. "Savhoran has been ill for some time," he said as he eased another plant from its pot.

"He said he was attacked." My voice sounded accusing,

which I hadn't intended.

Madera nodded. "His illness is a result of that attack."

I swallowed and stabbed my trowel into the dirt. "Will he get better?"

He sat back on his heels and sighed, looking at the plant in front of him. "He will never be free of this illness. He will find ways to cope, but it will always be with him."

Sounded like AIDS. My throat tightened up. I went back to digging.

It wasn't fair. I find a guy—a wonderful guy—who actually likes me, and now this. Not fair.

"The illness is...rare," Madera said. "It has not been studied."

I moved to the next row, frowning. Something wasn't right. Things didn't add up, but I couldn't figure out how.

"Some day there may be a cure, but for now, he must learn to live with it."

"How can I help?"

Madera stopped working and looked at me. "Truthfully, the best thing you can do for him right now is leave."

But he *liked* me! He said he was lonely!

"Why?" I said in a choked voice.

"The disease has just become active. I cannot really explain it to you, but he needs to be away from people just now."

I went back to digging, blinking back tears. "Can I come back?"

"I don't know, Amanda. I wish I had better answers for you. It will take a little while."

Dammit, dammit, dammit! Not fair!

"I think that is deep enough."

I looked at the hole I had made, twice as deep as the others. Shit.

I put down the trowel. "I'm sorry."

He came and knelt beside me, gently laying an arm across my shoulders. "So am I."

I lost it. The sobs just came shuddering up and I couldn't hold them back anymore. Madera gathered me into his arms and let me bawl all over him.

After a while I was cried out. He kept holding me until I sat up, wiping my eyes with my hand. He then produced a handkerchief—a real, cloth handkerchief—and gave it to me.

"Thanks."

I mopped my face and tried to pull myself together. Madera went back to planting, scooping some of the dirt back into the monster hole I'd made and setting a baby plant on top of it. After a while I shoved the soggy handkerchief in my pocket and picked up the trowel again.

We finished the planting in silence. Madera gave me the hose while he gathered up the empty pots. There was something soothing about the gently flowing water, the young, green things we'd put in the ground. When all the plants were watered we went back into the house.

Len had made some sandwiches. I was surprised at how late it was—almost noon—and that I was actually hungry. I pulled off the work gloves to wash my hands, and the band-aid came off with them. I started to cuss, then realized my finger didn't hurt.

The cut was healed. Hell, it was *gone*. I couldn't find it at all.

I looked around for Madera, but he'd slipped away, probably to check on Savhoran. Len beckoned me over to the table, and I gave in.

I had intended to challenge her about why we were leaving early, but after what Madera had said, I understood it. Was not happy about it, but understood.

If the best thing I could do for Savhoran was leave, then I'd leave. I wished I could say goodbye, at least. It hurt to just go.

Caeran arrived as we were finishing lunch; I heard Len's car pull up to the front of the house. Amazing how quiet it was out here.

I went to my room to collect my bag and met Madera on the *portal* carrying it out. I glanced past him toward Savhoran's room. The door was shut. Nothing to do but follow Madera to the entryway.

Len was there with her bag, talking to Caeran and one of his cousins. The cousin looked at me, smiled briefly—Nathrin, I thought—then said something to Madera and went through the door into the *plazuela*.

Caeran looked worried, but greeted me with a smile. The four of us went out to the car. Caeran and Madera put the bags in the trunk, then it was goodbyes all around.

When Madera came up to me, I held out my hand. "Thanks for your hospitality."

He took my hand and clasped it with both of his. "Be safe."

His eyes were blue, I noticed. Filled with kindness and regret.

"Thanks," I said, and got in the back seat before I could make a fool of myself again.

The back seat was my territory, safe from prying eyes. I buckled in and hugged myself and didn't look back as we drove away.

We drove for a long time along one side of a big, empty field on the right and a fence on the left. Madera's property must be huge.

Crazy to be leaving like this. Poor Caeran had been driving a lot—and I knew for a fact that he hadn't gotten his license until a few months before.

Somewhere past Mora I fell asleep. Woke up when we stopped for gas in Las Vegas. I went into the convenience store to pee, and picked up a soda after eying the ice cream.

While I was waiting in line to pay, my gaze drifted across a rack of newspapers. An *Albuquerque Journal* had a big black headline:

"CAMPUS KILLER RETURNS?"

= 4 =

I picked the paper up and started reading the story. "A man's body was found on the UNM campus early Friday morning, apparently..."

"Is that all for you, miss?"

I looked up at the cashier, then nodded and put the paper and my soda on the counter. I hadn't bought a newspaper since my pet parakeet died when I was in middle school.

I pocketed my change and went back to the car, where I read the news story until we pulled out. There was a picture of the victim—nice looking guy, vaguely familiar—and one of police tape tied around some trees. I skimmed the story for details.

The dead guy was a grad student. He was found by the duck pond, throat slit and bled out. My gut twisted into a knot; that pond was right next to the library where Len and I worked. The library where she'd seen the campus killer last fall.

Except she'd said he was dead.

Len got in the driver's seat and put on some music, then pulled out and got back on the highway. Reading in a moving car always made me sick, so I put the paper on the seat beside me. I'd read enough.

I watched the scenery go by, puzzling about the killer. My thoughts went around and around, and finally I gave up in favor of a less gruesome and, to me, more interesting subject: Savhoran.

I liked him enough to want to see him again, whenever he got well enough. I definitely was not just going forget about him. I decided to write him a letter and enclose it in my thank-you note to Madera. Spent the rest of the trip composing it in my head.

None of us were hungry when we got to Santa Fe, so we continued on home to Albuquerque. By the time we hit the outskirts of town I was starving. I leaned forward.

"Hey, you guys hungry? Dinner's my treat."

Len glanced over her shoulder at me. "You don't have to do that."

"I want to. It's a thank-you for taking me up to Madera's."

"You didn't get to enjoy it much. I'm sorry about that," Len said.

"At least I got to see it. You were right about Madera's place. It's wonderful. So what do you say? Dinner?"

They were silent for a moment, then Len said, "Sure. Where do you want to eat?"

We ended up at Pappadeaux, a great guilty pleasure, best when you're very hungry. I ordered my usual huge platter o' fried stuff. Len ordered the planked fish special and Caeran got a salad. In a fit of self-indulgence, I splurged on a fondue appetizer.

I'd brought the paper in with me. After we ordered, I laid it on the on the table in front of them.

"Talk to me."

They traded a long look, then Caeran turned to me. "Yes, we believe that was done by the person you saw."

A chill ran down my back. I swallowed. "And?"

"And that's why we took you up to Madera's," Len said. "These guys are serious hunters. He could have tracked you down."

I still had trouble buying that, but I let it pass. "Why are we back in Albuquerque, then?"

They didn't answer, and neither of them would look me

in the eye. I started drumming my fingers on the table top.

"The killer probably won't strike again for a while," Caeran said, looking uncomfortable.

"And you wanted to get me away from Savhoran?"

Caeran frowned. Len met my gaze.

"Yes, but only because he's so ill. It's not that we don't want you to be close to him. It's just that right now he can't..."

I waited, but she didn't finish. "You're telling me he can't see anyone? Or he just can't see me?"

"Anyone," said Caeran roughly. "Even staying with Madera is a risk. It is likely he will leave once he has adjusted."

Leave? No!

"Adjusted to what?" I demanded, panicking. "What is this disease, anyway? It doesn't sound like anything I've ever heard of."

"It isn't."

"Well..." Len said, then the waiter arrived with our drinks and some bread.

I sucked down half my soda and pulled a chunk off the loaf of hot bread. I was mad, and more than that I was scared that I'd never see Savhoran again. I had wild thoughts of going back to Madera's on my own, except that it would probably piss everybody off.

"Why don't you come stay with us for the summer?" Len said, helping herself to bread. "It would save you some money on the room."

"I'm not a mooch."

"Then buy some groceries. What do you say?"

It was tempting. I loved their house, and they did have a spare room. Len used it for an office, but there was a bed in there and it was a lot nicer than my dorm room. I'd crashed there on New Year's Eve.

"You're changing the subject," I said.

She sighed. "We're worried about you, Man."

"I'm fine."

"No, you're not. You're mad, and confused, and stressed-out. I'm sorry. The truth is..."

"There are some things you can't tell me. Yeah, I've heard that. Why not?"

"You would not believe us, for one thing," Caeran said.

"Try me."

I stared straight at him. I hadn't ever been that rude to Caeran before, but Len was right. I was frustrated as hell.

Caeran stared back, his eyes cold. I'd never seen him like this. He reminded me of his cousins with the names I couldn't remember, of the way they had looked at me like I was a gnat.

"How old do you think I am?" he said.

"Caeran, don't—"

He raised a hand and Len shut up. I saw her swallow before she looked down.

"Trick question?" I asked.

"No."

"I dunno...twenty-five?"

"Older."

"Twenty-nine."

"Older."

I didn't like this game. "Fifty," I said sarcastically.

The waiter was coming with our appetizer. Caeran's eyes narrowed and he lowered his voice to a murmur.

"Older."

The waiter arranged the plate in the middle of the table and said something cheery. Len answered and he went away.

Caeran was still watching me. No sign of joking in his face.

I leaned toward him. "Bullshit."

Something flickered in his eyes and I was suddenly

afraid. I had never, ever felt afraid of Caeran before.

"I was born in what you call the fourth century," he said.

Len gave a little sigh and dipped a piece of bread in the fondue. I didn't know whether to yell or get up and leave. She could have at least defended me.

"You don't believe me," Caeran said.

"Give me a break."

He shrugged. "I cannot explain if you refuse to accept ideas that are outside of your comfortable beliefs."

"Fine. You're sixteen hundred years old. You don't look a day over fifteen hundred."

"The person you saw at the blood center is probably older than I."

I didn't have a snappy comeback for that. I grabbed a piece of bread and swirled it around in the fondue.

"He—or she, it may very well be a female—is not human. Neither am I."

I looked at Len, wondering when she was going to tell him to quit. She just smiled and gave a little apologetic shrug.

"OK," I said, "setting aside that you're a Vulcan, how do you know that creep is one too?"

"Because we know the way the alben hunt. That student —" he gestured toward the newspaper "—died at the hand of an alben. My kindred and I were trying to find her, but it will be a few days now."

I swallowed a bite of fondue. "Oh? Why?"

"Because she is sated."

I stared at him, trying to work out some way that could mean something other than what it sounded like. "Sated?"

"The alben hunt for food."

"That guy wasn't eaten."

"No," Caeran said with the air of a parent patiently talking to a kid. "He bled to death."

Meaning the alben or whatever had drunk the blood. "But the article says the ground where he was found was steeped in blood."

"Yes. How many pints of blood are in the human body?"

Dammit. They'd just told us that at the blood donor center. "Ten."

"More than one person's stomach would hold."

My stomach informed me that this was not an appropriate topic for mealtime. Why was Caeran trying to gross me out? That was mid-school behavior. Certainly beneath someone over the age of fifteen. Hundred.

"She was at the blood center looking for prey," he said. "I went back and checked the register. The student she killed gave blood about the same time we did."

That was why his picture had looked familiar. I must have seen him at the center. I shivered.

"So we're either talking vampire or creepy vampire wanna-be. Right?"

Caeran leaned his elbows on the table and spoke softly. "I need you to set aside what you've learned from books and movies. This is real. The alben is immortal but she can be killed. She feeds on blood. She is—"

"Why do you think it's a she?"

"Because the alben often prey on the opposite sex. They use sexual attraction to disarm caution."

Oh, ew.

"So she seduced the guy and then drank his blood?"

Caeran looked tired. "I don't know. It is possible."

"OK, assuming I accept all this, what do we do now?"

Caeran glanced at Len. "You should come and stay with us for now."

"Why? The al—albino—"

"Alben."

"Whatever—she's sated, you said."

"For now. She may stay in the area, though. And she knows your scent."

Ugh.

"That's nuts. I can't stay with you indefinitely."

"You need not. Only until my kin and I find the alben."

"What are you going to do then?"

He looked down at the table. "Kill her."

He was flat serious. A chill sank into my gut. Caeran, pretty Caeran, Mr. Wonderful. Calmly determined to kill.

He must have picked up on my freaked-outness. "We will atone," he said sadly. "But we must keep her from harming others."

"Why not just call the cops?"

"She is alben. She is more powerful than any human."

"Oh, right. So, um—she drinks blood, she's immortal, and she's got super-powers. What else?"

"It isn't a joke, Man," said Len.

I raised my eyebrows at her. "You're telling me you believe this?"

"It's true."

"Uh-huh."

"We wouldn't be telling you about this at all if your life wasn't in danger!"

Len never yelled like that. She really did believe the fairy-tale crap Caeran was feeding me? Had he hypnotized her or something?

She turned to Caeran. "Just show her, all right?"

"Show me what?"

He shook his head, then looked at me. "You don't have to believe us. Just come and stay at our house for a while."

"I'll be safe in the bat-cave?"

"Safer than on campus."

I swallowed. He had me there.

The murder was too close to home. The campus killer last

fall had taken four students before the killings stopped. And yeah, they'd happened a week or two apart, as I recalled. Same MO.

Something clicked in my head and a bunch of pieces fell into place. "Wait a minute. You said the guy from last fall is dead."

"Yes," Len said.

I looked at Caeran. "And both you and Savhoran were injured last fall. Coincidence?"

"No."

"So you were injured by another of these monsters?"

"They are not monsters. They are alben. They are our kindred."

"*What?*"

"It's a disease, Man," said Len. "They're all the same race, but the alben have a disease—"

"That makes them immortal?"

"No," Caeran said.

"They're immortal to begin with," Len went on. "The disease makes them unable to digest much of anything but blood."

I watched them trade one of their long looks, then Len leaned toward me.

"That's why we had to leave Guadalupita. Savhoran has manifested the disease."

I gaped at her.

"I'm sorry, Man. We were all hoping he wouldn't get it, especially since Caeran hasn't..."

She shot Caeran a worried look. He laid his hand over hers.

"My wound was not as severe as his."

The last time I'd seen Savhoran, I had cut my finger. And he'd freaked out. Because seeing my blood made him want it?

My heart tried to flip over.

"No," I whispered.

"Amanda—"

"*No!*"

I jumped up, unable to sit still, unable to bear what they were telling me, even if it was just a cruel joke. I headed toward the entrance, walking, then running.

Faces blurred by: surprised waiters, curious customers, the hostess looking dismayed. I couldn't stand any of them, I had to get away from the crazy things Len and Caeran were telling me.

Vampires. Immortals. A disease that had struck Savhoran

—

No!

I ran out the door and down the steps to the parking lot. The Sandias were pink; the sun was down. I turned away from the frontage road and headed toward the movie theater. I had a vague idea of calling a cab and waiting for it in the safety of the lobby.

I wasn't thinking very straight, and I was still running because I couldn't stand to stop. If I stopped I'd be able to think about what Caeran and Len had told me.

Saturday night; there was a fair amount of traffic. I crossed the street in a gap between cars and headed for the theater parking lot. As I picked my way over the landscaping a shadow separated itself from a tree and stepped in front of me.

I gave a little gasp and tried to go around the stranger, but I couldn't. It felt like something had grabbed control of my brain, frozen me where I stood.

The stranger chuckled, which pissed me off and terrified me both. With the fading daylight to the west blinding me, I couldn't really make out the face, and that scared me even more.

"I remember you."

= 5 =

The voice was quiet—a woman or a high-pitched guy. Not an ounce of warmth in it.

I started to shake, even though I couldn't move. The stranger took a step toward me, and a flash of light blinded me.

I thought it was lightning for a second, but the sky was clear. I heard a grunt and scuffling. When I could see again there was a fight going on. The stranger was grappling with...Caeran!

Another flash of light made me step back, which was how I discovered I was no longer frozen. I scrambled away from the fight, but I couldn't just abandon Caeran.

I picked up a baseball-sized rock from the landscaping. Stupid, but all I could think of. I held it in my fist, trying to decide whether to throw it or try to clock the stranger on the head with it.

I didn't want to get that close.

The stranger was shouting. In the same flowy language Caeran used.

My heart sank. It was true. They were the same, except for the blood-drinking part. I hoped.

Caeran didn't answer, he was trying to get a stranglehold on the stranger. I hopped from one foot to the other, looking for an opportunity to use my rock.

Squeal of tires behind me. I dove for the tree. It was Len's car; she jumped out and ran toward the fight.

Well, crap. I went back, bringing my rock.

Len had something in her hand. She was getting too close

to the fighting. I followed her, my heart pounding.

We must have looked like idiots, the two of us dancing around while Caeran and the stranger brawled. The stranger's hood had fallen back and the long white hair spilled loose. Caeran grabbed a handful and pulled, but the stranger kicked at the same time and Caeran went down.

Len jumped forward, arm outstretched. The stranger gave a strangled cry, let go of Caeran, and ran off, staggering all the way.

"Caeran! Are you all right?" Len went to her knees beside him.

He was coughing and wheezing. Len knew how to help him better than I did, so I kept an eye on the stranger.

He/she stopped stumbling and ran north across the parking lot to disappear behind buildings. A creepy feeling came over me and I looked away, trying to shake it off.

"I'm sorry!" Len said to Caeran. "Oh, I'm so sorry! Man, get my water bottle from the car, will you?"

I went to the car, which was sitting crooked against the curb, engine running. I switched it off and turned the flashers on, then grabbed the half-empty water bottle.

I wanted to get the keys, too, but I still had the rock in my other hand. I had to tell myself the stranger was gone—twice—before I could drop it.

I hurried back to Len and Caeran with the water and the keys. Spotted Len's pepper spray canister lying on the gravel.

I used to tease her about her obsession with carrying that thing everywhere. I never would again.

Len gently dribbled water over Caeran's face. It was getting dark, but I could see that his eyes were swollen shut and streaming.

He reached up but Len batted his hand away. "Don't touch your face. That'll just make it worse."

He caught her by the wrist. "The alben—"

"She's gone."

"It's a she?" I asked stupidly. "For sure it's a she?"

"Yes," Caeran said, and coughed some more.

"We've go to get you to a bathroom," Len said. "Can you stand up?"

Caeran took a couple of deep breaths, then struggled to his feet. Len pushed the empty water bottle into his hands.

"Hold this. It'll keep you from touching your face."

She helped him back to the car and buckled him in. I got in the back seat, then remembered I had the keys.

"Len." I held them out to her.

"Thanks. Where's the nearest bathroom?"

I pointed to the restaurant directly ahead. This made me think of food, which made me remember I'd run away from my dinner.

"Oh, jeez! I meant to pay for Pappadeaux—"

"We took care of it," Len said, driving to the parking lot ahead.

It was a family chain, decent but nowhere near as wonderful as Pappadeaux. The host listened to Len's explanation, offered to call 911, and escorted her and Caeran away. I kicked my heels in the lobby waiting for him to come back.

The adrenaline was wearing off, and I remembered how it had all started. It seemed really stupid now that I'd run out into the theater parking lot by myself. Not that one usually expects to get attacked.

It was my fault that Caeran had gotten sprayed, kind of. Sort of. Yes, it was my fault for running out alone when I was vampire bait. From the perspective of having just experienced things that couldn't be explained, the warnings Caeran and Len had been trying to give me now made a lot more sense.

I felt bad about Caeran getting hurt. I felt worse about

what they'd told me. Savhoran had this disease, this vampire albino whatever, and maybe I'd never see him again.

That hurt to think about. To fight off crying, I picked up a menu and looked over it. I didn't really feel like eating, even though I'd been starving earlier. But I owed Len and Caeran a meal, so I chose a couple of sandwiches and a salad, and when the host came back I asked about ordering them to go.

Len and Caeran showed up before the food did. Caeran looked a lot better, almost normal. I was surprised because I'd heard that pepper spray lasted a while; it was supposed to incapacitate you for a good half hour. I thought about the stranger running away from the parking lot, stumbling at first but then doing a lot better.

"I'm sorry, Caeran," I said. "It was stupid of me—"

"It's all right," he said.

"Guess you believe us now?" Len said.

Ordinarily I would have called her on that snark, but she was right. I just nodded.

A waiter brought two carryout bags. I'd already paid for the food, so we took it out to Len's car and drove to their house. We didn't talk on the way.

We parked in their tiny driveway and Caeran got the luggage out of the trunk, including mine. Apparently I was staying for the night, at least.

He carried his and my bags into the house while Len got her bag and I brought the food. I heard Caeran's voice as I came up to the door, and saw one of his cousins in the living room.

"Go ahead and take those into the nook," Len said to me.

The nook was the tiny excuse for a dining room adjacent to the kitchen. They had made it beautiful, with plants and lace curtains and a gorgeous table that I now recognized as Madera's work. I put the food on it and sat in one of the chairs, staring out the window and remembering my abbreviated visit to Guadalupita.

Len came back and started fussing, bringing glasses of water and putting on a pot of tea. Since she'd met Caeran she'd become a tea drinker.

Caeran was still talking with his cousin, in their language. And what language was it, I wondered? Transylvanian?

I pulled the cartons out of the bags, and Len brought plates and silverware and napkins. Cloth napkins. Those were new, too. Madera's influence?

Len started opening the cartons. "Oh, good, you got a salad."

"I wasn't sure if Caeran would want anything."

"Salad's a good choice. What else have we got here?"

I couldn't stand her cheeriness. It had a false note to it.

"I'm really sorry—"

"It wasn't your fault, Man," Len said, putting the sandwiches and fries on plates. "But we just need to explain to you. It's more important now for you to know what we're dealing with. You want the fish or the chicken?"

"I don't care."

Len took the fish sandwich and gave me the chicken. I still wasn't hungry.

"Caeran's one of them, too?" I asked.

"He's not alben," she said sharply.

"But he said they were the same race—"

"They are. 'Alben' is what they call the ones who have the disease."

"Then what are the rest of them?" Not human, I knew.

Len gave me a speculative look. "They're ælven."

An hour or so earlier I would have scoffed. I didn't dare, now.

"Elves? They're *elves?*"

"Shh. They prefer 'ælven.' I know it seems crazy, but just

go with it, OK?"

I picked up a fry from my plate and took a bite. My stomach sent positive signals, so I nibbled a couple more. The salt tasted good. I still couldn't bring myself to pick up the sandwich.

Elves and vampires. I would wake up soon, now, right?

"They're immortal," Len said softly. "Caeran says he's actually the youngest of them. The ones here, I mean. Him and his cousins."

"And Madera."

"Madera's older than any of them. He's been here since Spanish colonial days."

Sure, why not? It explained the hacienda.

Something niggled at my memory and I frowned, trying to catch it. "Is Madera his real name?"

"Uh, no. It's the name he took when he came here. His real name is Madóran."

That rang a bell. I could hear Savhoran's voice saying that.

The front door closed. A second later Caeran came in and joined us. He reached for the nearest glass of water and chugged it down. Len pushed hers over to him and took his empty glass to the kitchen.

"Um," I said. "Thank you for saving me."

Caeran looked at me as he put Len's empty glass down. "You're welcome."

"Nice of you to risk yourself for someone who's not going to live very long.."

He gazed at me and his eyes softened. "You are a friend. It doesn't matter how long you will live. As long as you are here, I am your ally."

That gave me a warm feeling that I wasn't sure I deserved. I looked down at my plate. "Thanks."

Len came back with Caeran's glass and a pitcher of water.

"Where did Bironan go?"

"To find the others. They will go back to the theater and try to track the alben."

He glanced at me as if expecting a smartass remark. I was about as far from wisecracking as I could get.

The others must be his other cousins. He'd brought four of them down here, then brought Nathrin back to Madera's. Madóran's.

So there were three here still. I thought of them tracking down the alben and hoped they'd succeed.

"Amanda, please stay here with us for now," Caeran said. "That will make it easier to protect you."

I pressed my lips together and nodded. "OK."

"And please do not leave the house alone." He looked at Len. "Nor you. She will be hunting you, too, now."

Len sighed and nodded. "Sorry I screwed it up. I was just trying to help."

"You did help. She had the better of me." He took her hand.

I pushed my fries around on my plate, suddenly missing Savhoran.

"Stay together for now, if I am not with you," Caeran said. "I would take you both back to Madera's, but..."

I looked up. "Take Len back. She should be safe. Not her fault I can't go."

"I want you both where I can watch over you," Caeran said gently.

That made me feel small. I bit back a snide comment. If it hadn't been for Caeran, I'd probably be dead.

I ate a few more fries and listened to them making plans. They would go with me to my dorm tomorrow and collect up my stuff. Whatever didn't fit in their spare room would go in the shed out back.

I tried to work up some indignation about their high-handedness, taking over my life like that, but the truth was I was grateful. The thought of living in the dorm over the summer with a supernatural stalker prowling around made me shiver. My only other alternative was to go home. No thanks.

I stood up. "Guess I'll turn in. No, don't get up, Len. I can find the guest room."

The room looked like it had been hastily tidied. A candle was burning on Len's desk and my bag was sitting by the bed. I put the bag on top of a banker's box by the wall and took out my toothbrush and all that. Then I sat on the bed and cried a little. The day had been stressful to say the least.

How many times had I screwed up, just that day? I didn't want to think about it.

I got ready for bed and failed to sleep, haunted by the memory of being taken over by the stranger I now knew as the alben. I gave up when the sun started glowing through the curtains, and got up to look for breakfast, being actually hungry by that time.

Two of Caeran's cousins were in the living room. I said "Hi" as I passed through on the way to the kitchen. Couldn't shake the feeling they were watching me like I was a bug.

Len's fridge looked like Mr. Healthy eater did the grocery shopping. I was longing for a cinnamon roll, but the closest I found was some wheat bread. I put a couple of pieces in the toaster. At least Len still had butter.

I heard the front door open, then Len and Caeran came in. They joined me at the table and Len set a pepper spray canister in front of me.

I grimaced. "Do I have to?"

"Yes. I have one, too, and we got a couple of spares. They'll be in the laundry room cupboard."

"Isn't there any other way to stop them?"

Len raised an eyebrow. "Garlic, maybe? A lot of that is

myth, Man."

"What about sunlight? Will that get them?"

She glanced at Caeran. "It'll give them a rash, but that's about it."

She showed me how to use the spray. I put it in my pocket, hoping I'd never need it.

When I'd finished eating, Caeran went with me and Len to campus and emptied out my dorm room. I turned in my key and put in a request for a similar room come August, though thinking about school seemed surreal when I had a homicidal immortal stalking me.

For a couple of weeks things were quiet. Caeran or one of the others escorted me to and from work. Gradually I learned to tell his cousins apart and remember their names.

Caeran insisted that we stay in at night, so I set up my flat screen TV in the living room and started watching movies most nights. Len usually watched with me, and occasionally Caeran or one of his cousins joined us. I put on *Fellowship of the Ring* one night, just to see how they'd react. They seemed to find it funny; there was a lot of chuckling and comments in their language that they wouldn't share with me and Len.

Len got the job she wanted in the medical lab. "You should apply for one, too," she told me over lunch the first day she worked there. "We could work together."

"Thanks, but I'm not into medicine. Think I'll stick with the library."

"Man, it's not just a job. It's a project. To help the ælven."

I paused with a slice of pizza halfway to my mouth. "Huh?"

She glanced at Caeran, then leaned toward me across the table. "Madóran has some ideas for a cure for the curse, but he doesn't have access to modern laboratory equipment. That's why I'm taking pre-med. I'm going to do the research."

"But it'll take years to get to where you can even start!"

She nodded. "That doesn't matter much to the ælven."

"It matters to you! You're committing a chunk of your life to this!"

She looked at Caeran and her eyes got soft. "Yes."

I stared at her, wondering when she'd gone nuts and why I hadn't noticed. Things that happen gradually can sneak up on you.

Len looked at me. "You could help."

"Uh....it's not what I had in mind."

Actually, I didn't have anything in mind. I hadn't decided on a major. I felt no strong ambition to be anything in particular. Independently wealthy would be nice, but failing a winning lottery ticket or getting a lot better at poker than I was, I needed to figure out a career. I'd toyed with the idea of business school, not very enthusiastically.

But medicine? That was a lot of work, and a lot of stress, and nothing I was interested in.

Caeran turned to me. "It would help Len to have company in this effort."

"So *you* help her," I said.

"I will, but it is human company I mean. She does not have that."

"Just think about it, OK?" Len said. "That's all I ask."

I held in a sigh. "I'll think about it."

~

Wherever I went, Caeran or one of his cousins was always with me. It got on my nerves at first, but I got used to it. Sometimes I got jealous looks from other girls on campus, and that reminded me that these guys—all of them—were freaking gorgeous.

Funny, but I wasn't that interested in them anymore. I kept thinking of Savhoran.

Finally I scrounged up the courage to write him a note, and bugged Len for Madóran's address. I kept it short. I said I was sorry he was ill, and apologized for distressing him. I understood that I couldn't be near him, and I'd love to hear from him if he wanted to write. Gave my email address and Len and Caeran's street address, wrote a cover note thanking Madóran, Botched one envelope before I remembered to write Madera on the outside, and stuck it in the mail before I could chicken out.

That night I turned the TV on to watch a movie, and the local news came up.

"The campus killer has struck again at UNM..."

I sat staring, my hand still aiming the remote at the screen, my skin crawling. The victim was another guy. The newscaster sketched the details, then a tape of an on-scene reporter came on.

Len came in from the kitchen and joined me on the couch. She was frowning.

"...discovered early this morning on the north golf course near Bratton Hall..."

I sat up. "Bratton Hall? That's near the medical lab, isn't it?"

Len nodded. Coincidence?

Caeran wandered in as the story was wrapping up. He watched in silence, then looked at Len.

"You should not go back to work."

"I can't quit," she said.

I muted the TV. "Maybe just take a leave of absence?"

She turned to me. "I haven't even worked there a month. They'd think I'm nuts."

Caeran came and sat beside her. "There will be other jobs. The risk is too high now."

Except it wasn't just a job. I gnawed the back of my thumb. "We're home before dark. All the killings happened at night."

Caeran shook his head. "The alben can hunt in daylight. She prefers not to, but it is not safe to assume she never will."

"I can't quit, Caeran," Len said.

They stared at each other, long and hard. Finally Caeran sighed and went out.

He was even more obsessive about watching us after that. No more just walking us to and from the car—when Len and I were out of the house, one of the cousins was guarding each of us at all times.

I started going a little stir-crazy. I taught the guys to play Texas Hold'em, and every night we weren't watching doing homework or movies I bugged them to play poker with me. Lomen picked it up fast and seemed to really enjoy it, and the others weren't bad. Len played too, though she wasn't a great player. Too timid.

I was starting to feel really claustrophobic. I had to take a stand somewhere. I was damned if I was going to let a stranger who wasn't even human shape my life, so at breakfast one morning I screwed up my courage.

"I'd like to play in a poker tournament. There's one Tuesday night at Sandia."

Caeran gave me his flat look. "It is too dangerous."

"It's a room full of people in the middle of a casino. You think the alben would go there?"

"It is better to stay home at night."

"Tuesday's my birthday. This is what I want for my present."

He frowned and turned his tea mug in his hands. "Lunch would be better."

"It's a weekday. We're working."

"Why don't we go to Sunday brunch?" Len said.

"Because I want to celebrate on my birthday. It's just one night, Caeran. Please? You can bring your whole family if you want. I know Lomen wouldn't mind—he might even like to enter the tournament."

He pressed his lips together. Len put her hand on his arm. He looked at her, then sighed.

"All right."

"Great! Thank you thank you thank you!" I was so happy I could have hugged him.

"Where is Sandia?" he asked.

"North end of town. Way north."

"Is it near the theater?"

"Not really."

"Going anywhere is a risk."

"But the alben is more likely to stay near campus, right?" I said. "She's done all her hunting there so far."

"Almost all," Caeran said, looking at me.

I remembered the movie theater parking lot, and shrugged away a shiver. If I couldn't go out for one night, with four ælven protecting me...

That night the guys came over, and I brought up the plan. Lomen agreed to it instantly, and asked me a bunch of questions about the tournament and the casino. He wanted to play too, which mollified Caeran a little. We'd be in the same room.

So that they wouldn't have to split up to watch us both, we decided Len would come along too. She didn't want to play, but she could stand outside the poker room and watch. Like most casinos, Sandia's poker room was in the back, not near the front doors.

I spent the intervening days getting excited about it, waffling between nervousness and anticipation. When Tuesday morning came, Faranin escorted me to the library. I liked him—he didn't look down on me. We were all getting to know each other a little better.

Lunchtime the drill was Caeran escorted Len from the lab

to the library, then we'd eat at the Student Union Building or one of the restaurants on Central. Since we planned to have dinner at the casino, we just grabbed a bite at the SUB.

Len was grinning when they got to the library, and she kept looking at me sidelong while we got our food. When we were all settled at a table I called her on it.

"What?"

She grinned again. "Caeran brought in the mail."

Caeran took an envelope out of his pocket and handed it to me. No return address; beautiful handwriting. Postmarked Guadalupita.

I looked up, hope burning in my chest. Len's grin widened.

"Happy birthday!"

I tore the envelope open. The letter was brief, and didn't say anything all that important. What was important was that Savhoran had answered me. I stared at his signature a long time before I even looked at the message.

"How's he doing?" Len asked.

"Um. He says he's adjusting. Madóran's helping. He's trying to plan how to live with his affliction."

Caeran raised his head. "Good. He is staying, then."

"At Madóran's? He doesn't say so..."

"That's not what he meant," Len said, glancing at Caeran.

Caeran didn't say anything, just stirred his salad around with his fork. Len looked at me.

"He meant Savhoran's not giving up."

"Giving up?"

"Many who fall under the alben's curse choose to end their lives," Caeran said. "It is one more burden than they can take."

It had never occurred to me that being gorgeous and immortal could be a burden, but the sadness in Caeran's eyes made me think again. I had enough regrets in my own life, short as it was. Multiply that by a couple dozen and I could see how it might weigh you down.

I read Savhoran's note again. It actually sounded cheerful when I took into account that someone in his position was a potential suicide. He was definitely trying to be upbeat.

He didn't say anything about wanting to see me again, which was understandable. I was just glad he had written at all. I put the letter back in the envelope and tucked it in my pack.

"So," Len said, "there's another lab tech position opening up. You should apply."

"Yeah? What did you do today?" I asked.

"Cleaned lab equipment."

"Think I'd rather shelve books."

"It would be easier for Caeran if we both worked in the same place."

"Excuse me? This is temporary." I looked at Caeran. "Just until you guys catch the alben or she goes away, right?"

He met my gaze. "I do not think she will go away."

"Doesn't she know you're going to—you know?"

His eyes turned cold. "She knows. She thinks she can overcome us. If she caught one of us alone, she would have a good chance of it."

Len squeezed his hand. I had a feeling there was more to it than Caeran had said.

I changed the subject, mentioning that a recent movie had come out on DVD. We talked about trivialities for the rest of the meal, then they escorted me back to the library.

"See you at four-thirty," Len said, giving me a quick hug.

The afternoon crawled. I re-read Savhoran's letter several times. Started thinking about what to write in my answer. I was more a text-and-email person, but probably Savhoran didn't have an address; I'd never seen Caeran or any of the others use the Internet. As long as he was responding, I'd write letters.

Len and Caeran, along with Lomen, who'd been watching outside the library, picked me up and took me home. The others had gone ahead to the casino, no doubt to scout things out.

I went to my room and put on one of my nice tops. Half my clothes were still in bags from the move; I needed to get a dresser. I brushed my hair and put it in a spangly clip.

"Happy birthday," I told myself in the bathroom mirror.

I was finally twenty-one. Woohoo.

When had I stopped looking forward to being legal? This whole thing with Caeran and his family had knocked me off balance.

I went out to the living room. Lomen smiled at me from the couch. I grinned back, starting to feel excited about the evening.

"Ready to take all their chips?" I said.

"Yes!"

"Oh—I forgot to warn you, it's best to bring cash for the entry fee." I felt a pang of guilt for not having mentioned this before. I didn't know what Lomen's cash flow was like, but he seemed unphased.

"How much is the fee?"

I winced. "Fifty dollars."

I'd saved up for mine. Lomen just shrugged.

"No problem," he said, smiling.

We drove over to the casino, girls in the front, elves in the back. Len parked underground and the four of us marched to the elevator in a tight group, with Caeran trying to look all directions at once.

We went to the poker room first so Lomen and I could sign up for the tournament, then met the other two cousins outside the buffet. I would have been happy to eat there but Caeran continued past it toward the elevators. I started to protest, and Len slid her arm through mine, grinning.

"Happy Birthday. We're eating at Bien Shur."

The casino's best restaurant, one of the most expensive in town. I glanced at Lomen again, hoping this wasn't going to hurt his pocketbook. He seemed unconcerned.

We rode the elevator to the top of the building. Caeran had reserved a table on the north side, by the windows overlooking a spectacular view of the mountains. He took a seat facing the entrance.

I opened my menu and gulped at the prices. Len caught my eye.

"Our treat," she murmured. "Order anything you want."

I was starting to wonder if Caeran was rich. I'd assumed he and Len were renting the house, but what if he'd bought it? And then there was Len's car, which she'd got last fall. It was used, sure, but it was a recent-model Subaru, much nicer than the elderly Saturn she'd driven before she met Caeran. I glanced at him and saw that he was talking with the wine steward, a nicely-dressed individual who looked like he was from Sandia Pueblo.

"Excellent choice, sir. One bottle?"

"Two," Caeran said, handing him the wine list. "We're celebrating."

The steward made a little bow before walking away. Caeran smiled at me. "In honor of your attaining legal age."

"Thanks." I looked back at the menu and decided what the hell. I'd order the filet, Oscar style. You're only twenty-one once.

The wine arrived—red and rich, best I'd ever tasted—and the party began. Much to my surprise, they all gave me presents. Len had got me some pretty sand-cast earrings and Caeran gave me a bracelet that matched them. The cousins gave me little nicknacks they'd made: a deer carved out of wood from Faranin and a leather pouch with a beaded design from Bironan. Kind of hippie gifts, but they were cool, and I really hadn't expected anything at all.

Lomen grinned and told me to look inside the pouch for his gift. I pulled out a heavy disc about two inches across. It was a coin in a plastic case.

I peered at it in the restaurant's atmospheric lighting. "Liberty dollar?"

Lomen nodded. "To protect your cards."

"Wow! Thank you."

I'd told him about card protectors, usually medallions or special poker chips. I had a lucky chip I used—it was in my pocket—but this beat it by a mile.

"You guys are the greatest," I said. "Thank you so much!"

I had to shove the gifts aside to make room for food. We ate and drank and ate some more. A third bottle of wine showed up, and I was feeling pretty happy. If only Savhoran had been there, it would have been perfect.

I took a sip of wine, musing. The other cousins were just as attractive as Savhoran, and had less baggage. Lomen was friendly, even. I really should be considering trying to catch one of them.

I really had no interest in doing that.

No help for it. I had a thing for Savhoran. Not smart, but the heart is notoriously un-smart. Otherwise there wouldn't be all those angsty hit songs.

Bironan picked up the wine bottle, offering with a gesture to refill my glass. I shook my head.

"Better not. Want to stay sharp for the tournament."

Actually, I'd probably already drunk too much, but oh well. I was having a really fine dinner with a table full of good-looking men. Well, elves. Heck, that alone was worth the fifty bucks.

I managed to save room for dessert. I knew Caeran didn't like sweets, and the other guys seemed indifferent, but Len agreed to share with me. We ordered something with chocolate and caramel—it came out looking architectural, taller than it was wide, and made of artistic layers and adorned with an orchid. Len was afraid to touch it, but I dove in. It was bliss.

Len excused herself to go to the ladies' room. Caeran frowned as she stood.

"Me, too," I said, and got up. My head was a little light from the wine. "Safety in numbers, right?"

The waiter arrived with the bill at that moment. Caeran glanced at Lomen, who rose and followed us to the bathroom. I felt kind of silly, but I also felt safer with him outside.

We did what you do, primped a little, and went back out. The guys were gathered by the elevator. They'd found a bag and collected my gifts into it. I took out the coin and stuck it in my pocket. Checked my phone; we had about ten minutes until the tournament started.

"Dinner was wonderful," I said in the elevator. "Thanks again for all the presents."

"You are welcome," Caeran said, smiling. "Happy Birthday."

"And the wine. That was great wine."

"Your majority is worth a toast."

"Majority?"

Len glanced at him. "That's what the ælven call it."

"You celebrate turning twenty-one?"

"Fifty, actually," Faranin said. "Younger than that is considered immature."

Whoa. Half a lifetime for me, if I was lucky.

I'd sort of almost forgotten that they were immortal. They seemed more normal now that I'd gotten to know them.

I glanced at Lomen. He winked at me.

I shoved my hand in my pocket and fingered the coin case. I'd have to look closer at that coin. I'd assumed it was a replica, but with these guys, you couldn't make assumptions.

Caeran and the others clustered around me and Len when we got out of the elevator. The clump of us made our way to the poker room. The maddening circus music of slot machines surrounded us. I found myself glancing at the people sitting at the slots, but the only white hair I saw was on little old ladies gambling away their Social Security checks.

People were gathering for the tournament: four tables, thirty-eight players. Lomen and I had drawn different tables. Len offered to hold my bag of prezzies, and Caeran and the others arranged themselves outside the room.

My bodyguard. I could wish they were a trifle less conspicuous, but oh well. It was nice of them to escort me, and I was going to get the most enjoyment I could out of the tournament, since who knew when I'd get a chance to play in another one. I hoped they wouldn't be too bored.

My nerves were jingling a bit. Normal for a tournament. I'd never won one, though I'd made the final table a few times, and even gotten in the money.

I found my seat and nodded to the other players at the table. I didn't come here often enough to get to know the regulars. A lot of them played every week, some several times a week. Must be nice.

The tournament began and I forgot about everything but the game. I took out the coin Lomen had given me and used it to cover my cards. Tried to do it the same way every time, even if I was going to fold the hand. Good practice to avoid giving tells.

A waitress came by offering drinks, and I ordered a Coke, hoping the caffeine would counteract the wine I'd had. I played tight for the first couple of rounds, trying to get a feel for the other players, hoarding my chips. There was one bully at the table, all-in a lot, trying to steal the blinds, but by the end of the second round he was out.

I switched my play, taking chances on a couple of middling hands that I would have folded earlier. One paid off with a straight on the river and I took a pretty nice pot, enough to keep me safe for a while.

After the third round it was down to three tables, with

the players who were short-stacked beginning to drop out. I glanced up and saw that Lomen was still in the tournament. Good for him!

On the next hand I was dealt pocket kings. I put my Liberty coin on top of them and tried to look nonchalant while I waited for my turn to bet. Two players called the blinds, then the guy to my right made a big raise, doubling the pot.

I bit my lip. If he had pocket aces I could be dead, but I had to try.

"All in," I said, shoving my stack forward.

Everyone else folded, and the guy who raised called me. We turned over our hands. He had Ace-queen spades.

The flop was jack-four-ace with one spade. Not good. The turn card was the king of spades, giving me three of a kind but also giving him a flush draw. I held my breath for the river card, praying it wouldn't be a spade.

Seven of hearts. Whew!

"Break," called the tournament director as I raked in my chips. The other players got up, a couple of them saying "nice hand." The guy I'd taken out had already left the table.

I stood and realized we were down to two tables. With the pot I'd just taken, I would make the final table unless I did something stupid.

Lomen came toward me. "Very good, Manda!"

"Thanks. You're still in?"

He nodded and gestured to the other table, where there were six stacks of chips. A couple more players down and we'd be at the final table.

I headed out to the casino, needing a bathroom break. Len gave me a little cheer as I joined her.

"Thanks. Come with me for a pit stop?"

"Sure," she said.

Caeran followed us and waited while we went into the

ladies room. I finished before Len and was washing my hands when a stall door behind me opened.

In the mirror I saw a dark, hooded sweatshirt. I turned and was trying to yell, but all I got out was a squeak before the freeze grabbed me.

She stepped right up to me. Tall—they were all tall—and her eyes were black. She smiled in a smug way, ran a fingertip underneath my chin, then took hold of my arm.

"Come along."

She turned me toward the handicapped stall at the back of the restroom. My body obeyed her even though I wanted to kick and scream. She had her hand on the handle when Len burst out of another stall.

I caught a whiff an instant before my eyes started streaming. The alben let me go and I dropped to the floor. I heard footsteps and stuff, but I wasn't really paying attention 'cause the right side of my face was on fire.

"Shit, I'm sorry," Len said, putting her hand on my shoulder. "Don't touch it. Let me help you stand up."

I got to my feet and she smeared liquid soap on my face, which made it hurt even more. I cussed and cried and she wouldn't let me rub it off.

"Touching it makes it worse. The soap will help, just leave it on there. Trust me, I've read all about this."

I cussed again. "Is she gone?"

"Yeah. Caeran and the others went after her."

Happy birthday.

~

They didn't catch her. Needless to say, I was in no shape to finish the tournament. Lomen had stayed behind, and once I could walk he escorted me and Len home. Caeran and the boys were still out hunting.

After an hour that felt like a year and several applications of dish soap, my face stopped hurting enough for me to open my eyes and leave the kitchen sink. Still hurt, but it was bearable.

Len looked at me with worried eyes. "Sorry."

"You're dangerous with that stuff," I said, gingerly pressing a towel to my face.

"It got her off you."

She led me out to the living room where Lomen was sitting in Caeran's chair. On the coffee table were my presents and a chocolate cake.

"Cake. Oh, I love you!"

Len grinned. "Love Lomen, it was his idea. Want some ice cream?"

Yes. I wanted all the ice cream in the world. I wanted to bathe in it.

I sat down and cut myself a huge hunk of chocolate. As I was stuffing it in my face, my gaze drifted to the prezzie bag.

"My coin!" I said around a mouthful of chocolate.

"I picked it up for you," Lomen said, digging the coin out of his pocket. "Here."

I swallowed and clutched it in my fist. "Thanks. Didn't want to lose this. It was bringing me luck."

Guess I should have taken it with me to the restroom.

Len got out another pepper spray from the stash in the laundry room, and made me show her mine.

"Much good it does me," I said. "She does her mind-control thing before I can get it out."

"Well, keep it anyway."

Lomen sat up. "Has she used the mind-control on you, Len?"

"No."

He looked pleased. "Perhaps she does not have the strength to control more than one human."

Great. Why did I always get to be first choice?

Len stuck *Back to the Future* in the DVD player and we all sat watching it and eating cake and ice cream. I resisted the temptation to rub the ice cream on my face, but I did have seconds.

We watched the sequel and then decided to turn in. Len wouldn't let me help with the dishes.

"It's your birthday," she said, putting soap on a dishcloth. "Sorry it wasn't more fun. You were doing so well in the tournament. I feel bad that you had to miss the end."

"Not like you planned it."

I tried to look like I didn't care. Apparently I failed, because Len dried her hands and then hugged me.

"And I'm *really* sorry you got attacked. That sucks. This wouldn't be happening to you if you weren't my friend."

"Not true. I might still have given blood that day."

She leaned back and gave me a skeptical look. OK, she was right, I wouldn't have.

"Well, I'm selfish," she said, "so I'm glad you're my friend. It'll get better, I promise."

"Right."

I turned to head for my room but Lomen was standing in the doorway watching us. "Did Caeran explain to you that you are under our clan's protection?" he asked.

"Uh...not in so many words. You have a clan?"

"We have been remiss. May I tell you about us? I will answer any questions as well."

"Um. Sure, I guess."

He led me back to the living room and sat in Caeran's chair again. I perched on the end of the couch, feeling nervous. Usually the cousins ignored me.

"We are members of Clan Greystone," Lomen said. "It is like an extended family. We are cousins in the sense that we are blood relations, but not necessarily as close as what you call first cousins. There is also the complication that some of us are much older than others. Faranin was a friend of my father's father. Do you see?"

"Yeah."

"We live by a creed, a code of honor. The alben do not follow it, so we have been in conflict with them for many centuries."

"Could they follow it if they wanted to?" I asked.

"Yes, but few do. There was once a clan made up of folk who were afflicted with the alben's curse and still followed the creed. They are gone now."

"Why?"

He grimaced. "Many were killed in a fight with the alben around the time of Herodotus. After that they were too few to attract new members, and they gradually chose to return to spirit."

"New members? Are there new vam—uh, new alben all the time?"

"A child of two alben is alben. And some who fight them are exposed to the disease, as Savhoran was."

My heart gave a little squeeze. I'd been thinking about Savhoran a lot, and now I dared to ask a question that had been on my mind.

"If an alben bites a human, do they get the disease?" I stared at my hands, because I could feel myself blushing.

"Alben do not usually bite. That is a myth, along with the fangs. And no, humans are not affected by the disease."

So much for my chance at immortality.

"So Savhoran has no one to team up with," I said.

"He is still a member of our clan, unless he chooses to withdraw. You are also a member in a sense. When Caeran told you about us, it became his obligation to protect you, and as his clan-kin we share it."

"Huh? Why should you have to protect me?"

"It is part of the creed. We are...stewards of all lesser

beings in the world, and when a human becomes aware of us, it is our responsibility to protect her from the consequences of that knowledge."

I decided to ignore the "lesser beings" bit. "What sort of consequences?"

He smiled a little. "Being considered irrational by other humans, for example."

"Oh. Nut-case factor."

He raised an eyebrow as if he hadn't heard that term before. "Also, you have come to the attention of an alben who is now hunting you. We are obligated to protect you from her."

I nodded. Couldn't pretend I wasn't glad.

"Hard to catch, isn't she?"

His face got serious again. "She is powerful, and she poses other dangers to us. Do not worry, we will stop her."

I could think of one other danger off the bat: she could infect them. I wondered what else.

"Do the alben have a clan?"

Lomen shook his head. "They tend to operate alone, or in mated pairs. Too many hunting in the same area attract notice."

Yeah. I wondered how many serial killers were actually alben.

"Do you have other questions?"

"Yeah. If you guys are immortal and all, how come you're not running the planet?"

Lomen blinked and looked a little dismayed. Len came in from the kitchen and answered me.

"They breed really rarely, Man. Not like us." She sat next to me on the couch.

"Must be *really* rarely."

"Yes," Lomen said quietly. "To most of us, conceiving a child is something we dream of but never achieve."

"Wow," I said. "We sure don't have that problem. Can you have kids with humans?"

"Yes, but the children are mortal," Lomen said.

"Oh. Not good enough, eh?"

"That isn't it," Len said. "It's hard for them to watch their own children age and die. Caeran had kids with a human a couple of centuries ago. He kept track of them for a few generations, but they didn't know him, so it wasn't really like a family. He's still sad about it."

I looked at her with new understanding. She was lucky Caeran thought she was worth the emotional risk. I wondered if they were thinking about kids.

"The other problem," Len said, "is that ælven females have a hard time with childbirth. They can die."

"So can we."

"It's a bigger risk for them."

I looked at Lomen, who was watching us with a sad expression. "Guess it's not completely magical, then," I said.

He gave a small smile. "Everything has its cost."

I swallowed. My thoughts kept drifting back to Savhoran. I wished I could be with him the way Len was with Caeran. Selfish, I knew. Poor Savhoran had enough problems without worrying about a meepy mortal girlfriend.

I stood up. "Guess I'll call it a night. Thanks, Lomen."

"You are welcome. Happy Birthday."

Len helped me collect up my presents and take them back to my bedroom. I thought about how Lomen had enjoyed the cake and ice cream. Maybe it was just Caeran who was a health nut.

Len came in with me and set the carving and the pouch on her desk. "There's something else you should know about the ælven," she said.

"What?"

She glanced over her shoulder, then closed her eyes for a

moment. When she looked at me again her voice was a whisper. "They can hear your thoughts."

"Wha—"

"Shh!"

"What?!" I hissed.

She beckoned me over to the bed and we sat on it. "They have to be paying attention, and usually they have to be nearby, but they can tell what you're thinking. So watch the fantasies, OK?"

I tried to remember the last time I'd been fantasizing about Savhoran. Who was in the house?

"Shit!" I whispered.

"I can show you how to shield your thoughts."

I gave her a look, but decided it was best to be open-minded. "OK."

"You use white light. Ever done a guided meditation?"

"Uh, no."

She told me about it. Sounded woo-woo but what the hell. It couldn't hurt. We said good night, and I did the white light shield, then I took out Savhoran's letter.

There was no hint in it that he wanted to see me again. No promise of anything for the future. I went to bed and cried myself to sleep.

After that, I was nervous about being around the cousins. Kept wondering if they were listening in on my thoughts. Not that I was all that entertaining, but it gave me the creeps to think they could hear every little stupid idea that went through my brain. It didn't help that they never let me leave the house alone, and there was always at least one of them with us at home. I practiced the white-light thing every day, whenever I thought of it.

The only time I didn't have at least one of the ælven nearby was when I was at work, and even then they hung around outside the library. I didn't complain because I knew they were protecting me.

Every now and then I noticed one of them watching me —not just watching over me, but looking at me as if they were thinking something. Caeran did it most of all.

I wrote Savhoran another letter. I was careful not to plead or show any expectations, but I wanted to let him know I still cared. If we stopped corresponding it wouldn't be my doing.

I kind of regretted thinking that, because he didn't answer. After a couple of weeks I got really antsy, then I got depressed. I told myself it was for the best, but that wasn't any comfort.

~

One night we were all having supper when Caeran made an announcement. "I would like to celebrate Midsummer."

I stared at him, trying to figure out what he meant.

"Summer solstice," Len said. "They celebrate the solstices and equinoxes."

"Oh. You mean like religion?"

"Sort of. Closest thing we have to it is paganism."

Caeran glanced at her. "Paganism is based on what we taught humans long ago."

"So are a lot of our customs," Len said.

"But not all."

She smiled at him. "You going to tell them?"

A slow smile spread on his face as they gazed at each other. "Shall I?"

Len turned pink, which she rarely did. Caeran cleared his throat.

"Len and I intend to cup-bond at Midsummer."

Mixed reaction from the cousins. Faranin frowned a little; Lomen smiled and congratulated them. I sat wondering what a cup-bond was.

"It is a promise of fidelity for a year and a day," said

Bironan.

Dammit. Forgot to shield.

"OK," I said. "So, a short-term marriage?"

"In a sense, yes," Caeran said. "We do not have marriage —that is a human custom. Our equivalents are the cup-bond and handfasting, which is a life-long commitment."

"No divorce, huh? All or nothing?"

He nodded. "That is why we have the cup-bond. It is a way to try commitment without being bound to it forever."

I remembered Len telling me he'd been married—to the human mother of his children—back in the 1700's. So ælven *could* marry, except I figured they considered it life-long, like handfasting.

"Well, congratulations," I said. "So Midsummer will be a party?"

"Yes."

Caeran smiled at Len again, and I looked down at my plate. I was happy for them, but wished I could be as lucky. I still missed Savhoran.

Funny how you can get attached to someone on pretty short acquaintance. Maybe it's true that absence makes the heart grow fonder.

I picked at the rest of my supper and listened to them making plans. The solstice was on the following Wednesday, so Len and I would be working. Caeran asked Faranin and Bironan to watch us while he and Lomen set up the back yard for their Midsummer ceremony. I was mildly intrigued, but it was ælven stuff and a lot of it I didn't understand. Still, it was something to look forward to.

I didn't ask if they were going to invite anyone else. They never had other humans over to the house.

Funny thing was, I didn't miss my other friends. None of them were as close as Len.

The cousins were strange sometimes, and they tended to

take everything too seriously (except Lomen, who occasionally cracked a joke), but they were OK companions. I'd gotten to where I wasn't constantly comparing myself to them and coming up short.

Wednesday rolled around and Caeran drove me, Len, Faranin and Bironan to campus. I told Len I had stuff to do and asked if she'd mind not meeting for lunch. She probably guessed what I intended, but this was my only chance.

When my lunch break came, Bironan met me at the library doors. "Mind if we run an errand?" I asked him.

He frowned. "What errand?"

"I want to get Len and Caeran a present. Just at the liquor store—we can walk and be back by one."

He shrugged and fell in beside me as I started for Central Avenue. The day was hot and I hadn't thought of bringing a hat, so I'd probably get sunburned. Oh, well.

The liquor store had Gruet champagne—OK, sparkling wine, sorry French guys—a great New Mexico wine. I bought a bottle and stashed it in my backpack, then started back up the street with my escort patiently pacing me. I ducked into the campus pharmacy and bought a card, then picked up a junk-food sandwich and munched it on the way back to the library. Bironan said he wasn't hungry.

The afternoon kind of crawled by. I did busy work at my station and couldn't help remembering how last fall the other alben had come right into the library in daylight and abducted Len. I never saw him; Len said he'd worn a hooded sweatshirt pulled forward to protect his face. No reason why the alben girl couldn't do the same. I greeted Bironan with a grateful smile when he met me at the doors at 4:30.

We walked to the parking lot, but Caeran wasn't there so we walked on out to the street. I was just beginning to worry when I saw Len's car coming toward us. I didn't mind squeezing into the middle of the back seat. Safety in numbers.

At home—funny, I was already thinking of it as home—I hurried into the kitchen and hid the champagne in the bottom of the meat bin under all of Caeran's lettuce. Pots were steaming on the stove top, and the smell from the oven made my mouth water.

There were voices talking in ælven out in the living room, and when I went out to investigate I saw Madóran standing there chatting with the others. Nathrin and a woman I didn't recognize but who was obviously one of the clan were there too.

Nathrin saw me hanging back and beckoned to me. He and the woman turned toward me.

"Mirali, this is Amanda. Amanda, this is Mirali, my partner."

Partner. OK, good thing I hadn't tried to go for Nathrin.

"Hi," I said, remembering not to offer a hand. Handshaking was a human thing. The ælven clasped arms instead, and they didn't do it that often.

"Hello," said Mirali.

"You guys come down for the ceremony?"

"Yes," Nathrin said. "Midsummer is one of our sacred days. It is important to celebrate with kindred."

I nodded like I knew all that. Mirali looked a little shy and I didn't want to pester her, so I turned to listen to what the others were saying. They had shifted to English; Madóran was explaining how he'd got a neighbor to drive them down from Guadalupita.

He noticed me listening and turned to me with a smile. "I am glad to see you again, Amanda."

"Thanks. It's a nice surprise to see you, too." I hesitated, feeling myself turning red. "How's Savhoran?"

His face went serious, and he took a second to answer. "The last time I saw him he was well. He has left my house."

"Oh." I was already blushing, so what the hell. "I wrote him a letter..."

Madóran nodded. "It arrived after he left. I kept it for him, but if you wish me to return it—"

"Oh, no, no. Not important. Just give it to him when you see him again."

If you see him again. I didn't want to say that.

I cleared my throat. "Would you like something to drink?"

By the time I fetched drinks for him and Nathrin and Mirali, I'd stopped blushing so hard. Everyone made themselves comfortable in the living room, sitting on the floor when they ran out of furniture. I played hostess until everyone had a drink who wanted one, then opened a soda for myself and drifted over to where Len was sitting on the arm of Caeran's chair.

She smiled up at me. I bent down to whisper, "So when does the ceremony start?"

"Sunset. There'll be a feast after."

Sunset. As in, night coming. I was surprised Caeran wanted us to be outside after sundown, but then, the yard was fenced, so it was pretty private. And we'd all be together.

Sunset would be late—this was the longest day of the year, I knew that much—which meant that dinner would be late, too. I thought about sneaking a snack to tide me over. Caeran picked up a bowl of nuts from the coffee table and passed it to me.

Thanks.

He smiled and kept on talking. I took a handful of nuts and put the bowl down, and worked on practicing my white light for the rest of the evening.

Eventually Caeran got up and went out back. I collected empty glasses and put them in the kitchen, then returned and saw everyone filing out the back door. I followed.

The yard looked beautiful. It was always nice—lots of shade from the trees and tall flowering bushes along the fences, so it was very private—but now it was pretty enough for a wedding. Paper lanterns hung from all the trees, and a circle had been drawn on the lawn with something white—chalk dust, maybe. Four poles stood spaced around the circle, each holding a lantern of colored glass and wound with ribbons of the same color: yellow, red, blue and green. I could just see the flames of the candles glowing through the glass.

I stood on the back porch staring at it all. The little fountain that Caeran had given Len for her birthday was running, and the sound of the water settled my nerves. The candle on the patio table was lit, flickering inside its glass globe. It was still warm, but a slight breeze cooled the air a little and brought me the smells of candle wax and green grass.

Madóran was standing beneath the yellow lantern at the east side of the circle. He had put on a long, gold robe covered with embroidery around the neck and cuffs, and held a staff that was beautifully carved and decorated with fluttering ribbons. The others gathered around him, and Len beckoned to me to come inside the circle.

I felt a little self-conscious, but I joined them. Fortunately none of them looked at me as if I shouldn't be there. Lomen even smiled, and Madóran gave me a welcoming nod.

Len came over and whispered in my ear. "I've been to two of these. They're lovely and simple. Nothing to worry about."

Everyone else quietly chatted while Madóran stood silent, staring west. Finally he raised his arms, lifting the staff high, and everyone shut up.

We all watched, standing still for a long time until Madóran struck the staff three times on the ground. He said something in ælven, then in English he added "Welcome, all, to this Midsummer celebration."

He turned around, raised his arms toward the pole with the yellow lantern, and said a bunch more in ælven. Then he started walking around the circle, and we followed him. At each of the other poles, he stopped and talked in ælven. Len whispered to me again.

"He's greeting the guardians of the four directions."

I nodded. I could handle that, if it didn't get too much weirder.

Pagans liked to dance naked, I'd heard. I wondered if that was one of the things they'd learned from the ælven. I wouldn't have minded watching the clan do that, but I'd have been too shy to strip down myself. Also, the yard wasn't *completely* private, and there were laws against indecent exposure. Whether these guys knew about them was another matter.

Madóran reached the yellow lantern again and turned around to face us. He said some more in ælven, then added, "This is the longest day of the year. From now until Evennight, the days will grow shorter. May we rejoice in the beauty of summer and the bounty of the harvest to come."

He finished with a little more in ælven, then beckoned Nathrin and Mirali forward. He said some more stuff—looked to me like a blessing—and I wondered if they were doing a cup bond too. Then Madóran held his hands over Mirali's abdomen and I got it. She was pregnant. Yes, a little baby bump there that I hadn't noticed before.

I looked around at the other ælven. All their faces were intense, more than they'd been when we were walking around the circle. They were family, and in that moment I saw that every one of them treasured the unborn baby that Mirali carried.

I guess if it's hard to get pregnant, you care a lot more when someone you know does it. Also, Mirali was the only female ælven I'd seen (except for the alben, who didn't count). I wondered if the male-to-female ratio was as skewed throughout the ælven population.

Madóran said something and they all answered in ælven. Nathrin kissed Mirali's cheek and they moved away, and Madóran beckoned to Len and Caeran.

It was dusk now and the sky was that glowing blue color that's so magical. The paper lanterns in the trees looked like full moons, filled with soft, golden candlelight. A bird twittered somewhere.

Faranin brought a goblet filled with probably wine, and gave it to Madóran. He held it forward, and Caeran and Len both took hold of it, their hands overlapping.

"I promise to be yours and yours alone for a year and a day," Caeran said.

Len repeated the words, and they each took a sip from the goblet without letting go, then kissed over it.

That was it. The ælven all cheered, and broke into laughter and talking. Music started up, and I looked around for the source. It was Lomen, playing a wooden flute. The others started clapping, and suddenly they were dancing in a circle.

If you think folk dance you'd be getting close, except I never saw a folk dance so intricate. Madóran took the goblet back from Caeran and Len and they jumped into the dancing, Caeran leading Len around and rescuing her when she got in trouble. The rest of them didn't seem to mind when she messed up. I felt a little jealous, because she had to have learned that dance before; it was too complicated to wing it.

Mirali left the circle, laughing. When Nathrin followed her she shook her head and shooed him back into the dance, then sat in one of the patio chairs to watch. Madóran joined her. I decided against being a third wheel, and instead leaned on the wall beside the fountain and watched.

Dancing in the glowing light of the lanterns the ælven were even more beautiful, which I wouldn't have thought possible. Caeran, who was usually so serious, was laughing and smiling as if he didn't have a care in the world.

I noticed one ælven standing outside the circle, watching the dancers. He was the only one not smiling, the only one with his hair pulled back. He sensed my gaze and turned his head to meet it. The skin across my shoulders tightened and I suddenly couldn't breathe.

It was Savhoran.

= 7 =

I stood frozen, scared to believe it was really him. For a second I thought I was hallucinating, then he smiled just a little.

Oh, man. If there hadn't been dancing partying ælven in the way I would have run straight to him. Instead I worked my way around the outside of the circle to where he was standing by the trunk of a tree. He watched me all the way, arms folded across his chest.

I stood staring up at him for a minute, then remembered to talk.

"Hi."

"Hello," he said softly.

"I didn't know you were here."

He looked down. "I was unsure whether I should come."

"Well, I'm really glad you did!"

His voice took on a wry note. "It is nice that someone feels that way."

I glanced at the ælven in the circle. "They're your family. I'm sure they're happy to see you."

He gave a small shake of his head and a sad smile. "Mirali is not, for one."

I looked across the yard and saw her staring at us. Of all the ælven I'd met, she was the least friendly.

"Why?" I said, half to myself.

"She is concerned for the safety of her child. I understand; I do not blame her."

I could see the pain in his eyes so I changed the subject. "How've you been? I've been thinking about you."

A lot. A lot a lot.

"I am...managing. It is difficult."

"I heard you left Madóran's."

"Yes. I am here now."

"In Albuquerque?"

He nodded. My first feeling was indignation, but I put a quick damper on that. I wasn't mad at *him*, just at life.

I thought of a million nosy questions, but knew better than to ask them. If he'd wanted to see me before then he would have; he knew where to find me. I had to assume he didn't.

"It is best for me to be near a large city," he said. "Less likely that my hunting will be noticed."

I didn't like the word "hunting," but I let it pass. "Do you have a place to stay?"

"Yes. Caeran found me an apartment."

So Caeran knew he was in town, and hadn't told me. Maybe Savhoran had asked him not to. That hurt.

The music wound up to a big finale and everyone clapped and cheered. Mirali and Nathrin stood up and said something to Madóran, then all three of them went into the house. When I glanced up at Savhoran I saw him biting his lip.

"Hey, you want something to...drink?" I asked, barely saving myself from a faux pas.

"No, thank you." He looked so unhappy I wanted to hug him, but I didn't dare.

"Is it getting any easier?" I asked, lowering my voice.

He closed his eyes. "Not really. I dislike living this way, but I have no choice."

I swallowed. "Do you miss the sun?"

"I miss a lot of things," he said, looking at me.

My stomach flipped over. Did he mean me, or just things in general? He looked so sad and lonely. I wanted to make him feel better but I didn't know how, and I didn't want to offend him.

He looked toward the house and I followed his gaze. Madóran had come back out, alone, and gone over to where Caeran and Len were talking with Faranin and Bironan. Lomen started playing the flute again.

"Oh!" I said, "I have a present for Len and Caeran—will you come in with me while I get it?"

Savhoran frowned. "Mirali is inside."

"I think they left. Anyway, you're not going to bite her, right? Come and keep me company?"

He looked reluctant, but he followed me across the circle and into the house. The living room was empty. We went on through the nook into the kitchen, where the turkey that had been in the oven was now sitting on the counter smelling even more wonderful.

"Have you talked to anyone? Tonight I mean."

"Only you."

I opened the fridge. "Well, you should say hi at least. I bet they'll make you welcome."

"If they do, it will be out of politeness. I am a danger to them now."

I looked up at him, arms full of lettuce. "I thought it wasn't that contagious? Madóran said it took intimate contact —"

"That is what we believe, but we have no proof. Many prefer to be cautious."

I unearthed the Gruet and stuffed the lettuce back in the bin. The smell of the turkey was making my empty stomach grumble. I carried the wine out to the living room, then stopped and turned to Savhoran.

"Len and Madóran are working on a cure, she told me."

"Yes, but it will take a while. I am not sure that I want to wait."

That scared me more than anything he'd said. "You're not alone," I said, too sharply.

He gave me another sad smile. "Thank you."

I couldn't stand it any more. I put the champagne on the coffee table and got in his face.

"Don't you quit on me," I said.

He looked startled. I threw my arms around his neck.

"Don't give up," I said into his shirt.

For a minute he didn't move, then he slowly put his arms around me. I had my face buried in his shirt and he smelled fantastic. My whole body was tingling. When he kissed my hair—so lightly—it sent a shock through me and I raised my head to look at him.

He stared back at me. The sadness had been chased away by a spark of something else—something stronger.

Yes. Oh, yes.

He kissed my forehead, then my cheek, then the corner of my mouth. Feather kisses; they drove me crazy. Finally he kissed my lips, and I kissed back with all the bottled-up feelings I'd had for weeks. I knew it was all right when his arms tightened around me.

"Guys! Get a room!"

We jumped apart just like in the movies, and I shot Len an angry look. She smiled as if she hadn't noticed.

"Hi, Savhoran! Good to see you, I'm glad you could come."

"Th-thank you."

He looked confused. I wanted to hug him again and soothe the worry away.

"Man, we need to set up the feast," Len said. "Will you help me?"

"Uh, sure." I looked at Savhoran.

"I should not be near the food," he said.

Len went on into the kitchen. I caught Savhoran's hands.

"Don't leave."

"I'm going to find Madóran. I have a question for him."

"Savhoran—"

He kissed my forehead again. *I won't leave without saying goodbye.*

I gasped, because suddenly I could feel him—not his body but his soul, I guess—and it felt *wonderful!*

He smiled and squeezed my hands before he let go. The sense of him faded at once, much to my regret. I watched him out of sight, then followed Len into the kitchen, stunned. She had put the turkey on a platter and was arranging roasted potatoes and carrots around it.

"Unwrap those casseroles, will you?" she said.

I stared at her. "He just talked to me without talking!"

She glanced up. "Oh. Cool, huh?"

"Does Caeran do that? Is that what you guys are doing when you make moony eyes at each other?"

"Heh. Yeah. You going to help or not?"

I unwrapped the casseroles: stuffing in one, noodles in a creamy sauce in the other. "How come Caeran never talks to me like that?"

"Well, it's kind of intimate, you know."

Yeah, I knew. I wanted to know some more.

"Do they talk to each other that way?"

She paused and frowned. "I don't think so. No, if they could do that then Caeran wouldn't need a cell phone. Could you get out the salad?"

I got the gigantic salad bowl from the fridge. We put all the food out on the table in the nook, along with bread, cheese, cranberry sauce, gravy, a couple more side dishes and a huge bowl of fruit. It looked like enough to feed a couple dozen people, and we were down to seven, not counting Savhoran.

I followed Len out back and while she was summoning

people to the feast I looked for Savhoran. He was over by the tree again, sitting with his back against it. I sat next to him and watched the others go in.

"Go and eat. You are hungry."

I looked at him, scared and excited at once. "Are you?"

He frowned. "No."

"Because if you are—"

"No! Do not say that—do not think it!"

"I would do that for you."

He gazed at me, sadness back in his eyes. "I would rather die than hurt you."

I swallowed, hoping I hadn't offended him. Maybe he heard that thought, because he smiled and touched my cheek.

"Go and eat," he whispered. "I will be here."

I did, because I was starving. I wanted to grab some food and bring it out to where Savhoran was sitting but I thought that might make him uncomfortable, so I cut a couple of slices of fresh bread and made an impromptu sandwich with some turkey, stuffing and cranberry, and stood in the corner of the living room scarfing it down.

The family was sitting on the floor and the furniture with their plates. Caeran had opened the champagne and shared it around. I shook my head when he offered me some. I wanted to keep my head clear so I wouldn't do anything stupid.

They were talking about some other place they had been, Europe maybe. Len had told me that's where they came from before they got to Albuquerque. Lomen was telling a silly story about tricking humans who were trying to track them down.

I felt out of place. They could say I was part of the clan all they wanted, but I still didn't feel welcome. Maybe they didn't like my interest in Savhoran. Or maybe they were uncomfortable having him at the party.

I swallowed the last bite of my sandwich, went in the kitchen and grabbed a soda, and went back outside. The candles were still glowing in the lanterns, filling the yard with soft light. The empty circle with the colored lanterns on four poles looked like some formal space now. I walked around it, not wanting to break whatever sacred energy filled it.

Savhoran smiled up at me as I sat beside him again. I sipped my soda, trying to think of something to say. The things that were most on my mind would be awkward to talk about. I settled for conventionality.

"How long have you been in Albuquerque?"

He hesitated. "Two weeks."

"Oh."

Two weeks and he hadn't contacted me. Maybe he wasn't so sure he wanted to see me.

He took the soda out of my hand and put it on the ground, then took me by the shoulders and kissed me.

I did want to see you. I tried to avoid it because I do not want to harm you.

And there it was again, all his pain and sadness. I clung to him.

You won't harm me.

He wrapped his arms around me. *I will try not to.*

You've been going out with them, haven't you? Hunting the alben?

Yes.

I took a sharp breath, because his anger had flared with that answer. He wanted vengeance, and the alben was his target even though she wasn't the one who had infected him.

We have a custom—it is something like your "eye for an eye." I will not rest until she is dead.

Nothing I could say to that.

I leaned my head on his shoulder and closed my eyes. I

was tired of being scared of the alben, tired of being lonely. It felt so good just to be held.

I woke up in my bed, alone. Sat up trying to remember my dreams, figure out whether they actually were dreams. I reached for my water glass and that's when I saw it.

A ring, just a plain band of metal, looked like gold. It was lying on top of a folded piece of paper on my nightstand. I held the ring in my hand while I read the note.

Amanda -

This ring was my eldermother's. It is very old. I give it to you now as a pledge of my affection and friendship. I do not have much to offer, but what I have is yours.

I will visit again soon.

Savhoran

I stared at the ring, wondering if he knew what a gift like that traditionally meant to humans. He had to, didn't he? Unless he'd been living in a cave all his life...

I slid the ring onto my finger, feeling goosebumps rise on my forearms.

It was gorgeous. It fit perfectly. I took it off and rummaged in my dresser for a chain to put it on. Too confused about what it meant; I'd wear it around my neck for now.

If an eldermother was like a grandmother, then that ring must be really freaking old. I fastened the chain and slid the ring into my shirt, trying not to wonder about its value.

The clock said I had half an hour to get dressed and get ready for work. No problem, I was already dressed.

Disgusted with myself, I changed and went to the kitchen looking for breakfast.

The three resident cousins were in the living room talking. Len and Caeran were drinking tea and eating scones. Caeran was almost as good a baker as Madóran, and the kitchen smelled heavenly. I helped myself to a scone and made myself a cup of instant coffee.

"Savhoran asked me to tell you he said goodbye," Caeran said.

"Thanks." I joined them at the table, ignoring the curious look Len gave me.

"He also asked for your cell phone number. I assumed you wouldn't mind my giving it to him."

"No, no. Thanks. He has a phone? Can I have the number?"

"Yes."

He must have anticipated the question, because he pushed a scrap of paper toward me. I stared at the number on it, knowing I shouldn't use it but desperate to have it anyway. I tried to look calm as I programmed it into my phone and then put the phone back in my pocket.

I did not want to go to work. I wanted to call Savhoran and invite myself over to his place. Bad idea.

Lomen was my escort du jour. I liked him because he had a sense of humor, and he didn't look down on me. He was practical, too. One day he made up a list of books he was interested in reading, and he had me check them out one at a time for him to read while he was guarding the building.

He came into the library with me that morning, because he'd just finished *Mein Kampf.* I dropped the book in returns. "What's next?"

"*War and Peace,*" Lomen said.

"Oh, man. You really ought to read that one on the Kindle."

He gave me a curious look. Not wanting to explain ebooks to him in public, I pulled the book for him and checked it out on my account. He hefted it and grinned at me.

"See you at lunch."

I smiled and went back to my station. Poppy, the goth who works the same shift as me, was looking at me.

"So you got a gorgeous boyfriend, too? Does he have any brothers?"

I racked a stack of data entry forms. "He's just a friend. No brothers that I know of."

"A friend you have lunch with every day. He looks like Len's boyfriend."

"They're cousins."

"Damn. Sure there aren't any more at home?"

I didn't answer, because I didn't want to lie and I sure didn't want to tell the truth. The cousins looked enough alike that Poppy thought she was seeing the same one all the time. No need to correct her on that.

I dove into the data entry and tried to keep from thinking about Savhoran every other minute. Didn't do so well on that but the work made the time pass.

Just before lunch, Steve Harrison came up to my station. Of all the students who hung around the library that summer, he was the best looking: slim but not skinny, blond with brown eyes and a smile to tighten your loins. He was almost as gorgeous as the ælven. Brilliant, too; he was carrying a double major in chemistry and physics and barely breaking a sweat. Unfortunately for us single girls he was also gay.

Maybe I wasn't a single girl anymore, I thought as I watched him walk up. A little happy shiver went down my spine.

"Hi, Steve. What can I do for you?"

"That book on isotopes come in yet?"

"Let me check." I looked up the record. "Nope. Yours is the first hold on it, though."

"Damn. I need it for a paper. Wasn't it supposed to be in by now?"

"Yeah. It's overdue."

"Gimme the guy's address."

"You're going to strong arm him? No, you're going to seduce him. Sorry, I can't give out that information."

"Will you call him?"

I leaned on the counter and flirted up at him. "What'll you give me?"

He looked sarcastic for just a second, then smiled a slow smile. "Have you chosen a major yet?"

"This isn't about my education. It's about your book."

"Try economics. You're a natural."

I straightened up and glanced over at Poppy. "I think I've just been insulted."

"No, I'm serious. You're good with numbers, and you get the big picture. You're a planner. Check it out. There's a 200-level course in the fall. You should consider it."

He was serious. I was touched; I didn't think he cared a rat's ass about me.

"OK, I'll look into it. And I'll call about the book."

Steve gave me his dazzlingest smile. "Thanks, sweetie. Later."

He headed up the stairs. Poppy came over to my end of the counter and leaned across it to stare at him until he was out of sight.

That was the most exciting thing that happened all morning. I called the delinquent borrower and left a message, then sent an email for good measure. Did my data entry, helped a few people with checkouts, and gossiped with Poppy.

At lunchtime I signed out and headed for the restroom, passing Steve on his way back down the stairs. I smiled at him but didn't stop to chat, as my need for the restroom was genuine.

It was empty, unusual for the lobby at lunchtime, even in summer. That should have warned me, but I didn't catch it.

Halfway to a stall, I felt the freeze coming.

= 8 =

Lomen!

I managed that, then I couldn't even think any more. I was breathing, my eyes were open, but none of it was under my control.

A hand grabbed my arm and pushed me toward guess where—the handicapped stall. I was turned around and shoved against the wall by my best alben girlfriend.

I could see her sweatshirt and her hands, but I couldn't move my eyes to look at her face. She pulled a knife out of her pocket. I was terrified, but since I couldn't scream I just wondered how she'd got it past the metal detector at the library entrance. Mind control, maybe?

She reached up and cut my neck right under my ear, then latched on and sucked hard. Lomen was right about the no biting. It only hurt a little, but I was scared to think she could be sucking the life out of me, in the women's restroom forgodsake.

The outer door opened. A girl screamed, then ran back out.

Door again, and Steve's voice saying "Amanda?" and then the door banging hard against the wall.

The alben let go of me and went out. There was yelling and scuffling and a masculine shout of pain, the door, running footsteps, then Lomen's voice: "Take care of her!"

And the door again. I blinked, realized I was unfrozen, and sank to the floor.

Steve pushed the stall door open wider. "Oh, shit! Amanda!"

He picked me up and carried me out of the stall, set me on the floor, grabbed some paper towels and pressed them against my neck. Then he took out his phone.

Even though I was free I was kind of in shock, and I just sat there listening to him talk to the 911 operator. Lomen wasn't there so I figured he'd gone after the alben.

I realized Steve was talking to me. "...going to be OK, there's an ambulance coming."

I looked at him, touched by his worried expression. "How did you know...?"

"I saw her follow you in and I didn't like the look on her face."

I blinked and nodded, making the paper towels rustle. "Thank you."

He smiled. "No problem."

Campus security showed up before the ambulance. They weren't a lot of help, but their presence was reassuring. They asked me questions I couldn't really answer, not without getting sent for a psych eval. I did the best I could with the plain facts.

EMTs came in, and Poppy followed them. Her eyes got huge when she saw me.

"Tell Dave I can't work this afternoon, OK?" I said. Understatement of the year.

She nodded and left, looking shook up. I, on the other hand, was perfectly calm. Funny how practical you can be in an emergency if the emergency is you. Other people get all the angst.

The EMTs cleaned me up and patched me up, then insisted on putting me on a stretcher.

"I can walk," I said.

The tech frowned at me. "Hold out your hand."

I did. It shook like an aspen leaf.

"You've lost some blood. We've got to take you to the

hospital."

My feeble protests were ignored. Steve continued in the role of white knight, fetching my pack when I asked him to and offering to follow the ambulance and meet me at the hospital.

"You'll miss your classes," I said.

"I'm not leaving you alone."

I was very un-alone, but I appreciated the support. At the hospital they stuck me in a bed in the emergency room and ignored me for a long time, and I was really glad to have Steve's company. The place smelled like hospital. Ugh.

I dug my phone out of my pocket and called Len. She answered on the first ring.

"Hi, Len—"

"Man! What's going on? Caeran took off like a bat out of hell!"

"I'm OK," I said. "I'm in the emergency room."

"You're hurt? Was it the alben?"

"Uh-huh."

"Is Lomen with you?"

"No. Steve Harrison is."

"So you can't talk. OK. Have you seen Caeran?"

"No."

"Did Lomen go to meet him?"

"I don't know. Maybe."

"They're chasing the alben."

"Yeah."

She was silent for a minute. "Caeran told me to stay here."

"I think that's a good idea," I said.

"But do you want me to come over there?"

"No. I'm OK."

"All right. Call me if anything happens."

"Same to you."

We hung up and I left my phone on the bed. I was tired, now that the adrenaline had worn off. I looked at Steve, who was watching me.

"Thanks," I said for the hundredth time.

He nodded. "Do you know that girl who attacked you?"

"Not really. I've seen her before, but that's all."

"She a student?"

"I don't think so."

"She had white hair—didn't the campus killer have white hair?"

"They never caught him."

"But there was a suspect. I'm pretty sure he had white hair."

And he had raped his female victims. I didn't feel like bringing that up, so I decided it was safest not to comment any more. I was tired of playing twenty questions. Fortunately a nurse came in before Steve could grill me again.

She took my vital signs and frowned at the blood pressure gage. Redid the cuff, frowned some more, then left.

"So why are you taking a double major," I asked before Steve could go back to interrogating me about the alben. "What do you want to be?"

"Really good at something lucrative."

"Pharmaceuticals?"

He wrinkled his nose. "I'd rather not."

"That's where all the money is."

"I'd rather do something like spacecraft engineering."

"Interesting. Not lucrative."

"Yeah, I know."

Lomen came in, looking a bit wild-eyed. There was a bloodstained gash across the right shoulder of his shirt. I couldn't help a gasp, which he ignored as he came to the bed.

"Are you all right?" he said.

I nodded. "Just waiting to be sent home."

"You should have that looked at," Steve said to Lomen.

Lomen turned and gazed at him. "Thank you for your help."

Steve eyes got a little wider. "Any time."

"Lomen, this is Steve. Steve, Lomen."

"Honored," said Steve.

Lomen nodded, then looked at me. "I am sorry."

"Not your fault."

"I swear to you she did not enter the building while I was there."

"Maybe she was there before you got there," said Steve.

Not a pleasant thought.

"Where's Caeran?" I asked Lomen.

"With Len."

That was good. I looked at my phone: two-thirty. I was tempted to call Savhoran, but he couldn't really do anything to help, and I didn't want to upset him.

The nurse came back with a doctor. Lomen faded back against the wall, and the medicos never even looked at him. They took my blood pressure again. The doctor frowned.

"Does your blood pressure normally run low?"

"Not that I know of," I said.

"Have you given blood lately?"

"Oh, yeah—about a month ago."

"And you lost some today. I'm going to give you a unit of saline."

"Is that necessary?"

"Yes."

He turned to the nurse and started talking medicalese, then they both went out. I looked at Steve.

"I guess you could go. Lomen will make sure I get home."

Steve looked reluctant, but stood up. "OK. Call me if I

can help with anything."

He gave me his number and I programmed it into my phone. I thanked him a few more times and he left.

I looked at Lomen, who was gazing after Steve, his face thoughtful.

"Maybe you really should have that cleaned up while you're here," I said. "It looks a little scary."

He glanced at his shoulder. "It is fine. Madóran is still in town. He can do anything it needs."

I wished Madóran was taking care of me instead of UNMH. Not that they were bad—I didn't say that—but I wanted to be home, not there.

The nurse came back with a bag, hung it on a rack above the bed, and installed the IV in my arm. She changed the bandage on my cut, then left me alone with Lomen.

"Did you catch her?" I said after a minute.

He shook his head. "She is fast, and she had a knife. We were unarmed."

I thought about the pepper spray Len made me keep in my pocket. Maybe all the ælven should carry it, too.

"She jumped onto a bus. We could not follow." He looked up at me, eyes worried. "Forgive me."

"Stop with the guilt, OK? It isn't your fault."

He sat in the chair and stared at the floor. "It was my responsibility to protect you."

"Well, you did. If you hadn't come in she wouldn't have run. And you got hurt trying to catch her, so you didn't fail, OK?"

He didn't look convinced, but he didn't mope anymore, at least not out loud.

It took forever for the bag to empty. Caeran and Len showed up just as the nurse was taking out the IV.

"You guys brothers?" she asked, looking from Caeran to Lomen.

"Cousins," Caeran said.

"Can I go, now?" I asked.

"We just need to do some paperwork." She checked my vitals yet again and noted it all down. "I'll be right back."

"Argh," I said when she'd left.

Len came to the bed and took my hand. "I'm sorry this happened, sweetie."

"What is it with that alben and bathrooms?" I said crankily. "That's twice now she's come after me in a bathroom!"

"It is a place where we cannot follow you," said Lomen.

"But why me? There have to be easier—um, choices."

"She considers it a challenge." Lomen looked at Caeran. "And she wants to hurt us."

"So instead of attacking you she goes after me? Pretty cowardly."

Lomen didn't answer. I wondered if cowardice was a concept the ælven understood, or if it was a human idea.

Half an hour later the hospital finally let me go. Caeran and Lomen stuck to me like burrs as we walked out to the parking lot. We got into Len's car and headed home.

I was starving by this time, so I made a beeline for the fridge, which was full of leftovers from the feast. I loaded a plate with turkey and stuffing and veggies and stuck it in the microwave, then opened a soda and chugged half of it while my late lunch was nuking.

The others all gathered in the living room. Madóran was there; I saw him look at Lomen's shoulder and say something to him. Didn't seem concerned about the wound.

I brought my plate out and sat on the floor since all the furniture was taken. I dug in while while Lomen filled the others in on what had happened at the library.

Madóran gave me a concerned look. "You should not return there."

"I have a job."

"Is it worth risking your life?"

Pushing library electrons around? Hell, no, but I didn't want to be pushed around either.

"You guys need a different strategy," I said. "So far you've been reacting to her moves. You need to take charge. You outnumber her."

"She is clever," Lomen said unhappily.

"We should move Len and Amanda out of the city until we catch her," Caeran said.

"Mirali must certainly leave," Madóran said. "I will take her and Nathrin back to Guadalupita. I would be happy to take Lenore and Amanda as well."

"Your friend's car will hold all of us?" Len asked.

"I will make other arrangements. A limousine."

I resisted the urge to whistle, and reminded myself that Caeran was rich. Maybe Madóran was, too. Maybe they all were.

"Has anyone called Savhoran?" I asked.

No one answered.

"It's his business too, right? I'll call him."

I got up and took my empty plate to the kitchen, then took out my phone. Pulled up his number and then hesitated. Would I just be causing him needless anxiety?

No, he was a part of the clan, so he needed to be in on the planning. I hit "send."

He answered on the third ring. "Yes?"

"Hi, it's me. Amanda."

"Amanda."

"Listen, I don't want you to get upset or anything, OK? Everything's OK."

"Then why would I be upset?"

"Well, um. We had a little incident with the alben today —"

"Where are you?" His voice was suddenly urgent.

"Relax, I'm at home. It's OK."

"Were you hurt?"

"Only a little."

A loud clunk made me jump. Sounded like the phone had been dropped.

"Savhoran?"

No answer. I thought I heard footsteps, then a door slammed.

Well, no one could say he didn't care.

I put my phone away and went back to the living room. Leaned against the wall, trying to think of a better way to catch the alben than just waiting for her to attack one of us.

"She doesn't like the sun, right?" I said. "So if you search for her during the day, maybe you'll find where she's hiding."

"We have already searched the campus and surrounding area in daylight and found nothing," said Faranin.

"Then we must broaden our search," Caeran said.

"What if—"

The front door opened. I turned and saw Savhoran, wearing a hoodie that was crooked like he'd put it on fast. He looked at me and his brow wrinkled with grief, then he caught me in his arms and held me so tight I almost couldn't breathe.

"It's OK," I whispered.

I am sorry, I am so sorry!

And I felt how sorry he was, and I wanted to make it better.

It isn't your fault. Come and join the discussion. We're planning how to catch her.

That worked. He let me go and took a step into the living room.

"I wish to lead the hunt."

He pushed back his hood and I sucked a sharp breath. His face was fried like he'd been in the sun for hours. He must have run to the house from his place—nearby, I assumed—but the hoodie hadn't protected him enough.

Madóran got up and went to him. Savhoran shook his head, but Madóran put his hands over his face.

"The sooner treated, the less harm."

The ælven murmured in their language, then Lomen stood. "Sit here, Savhoran. I will make tea."

Madóran and Savhoran moved to the couch while the others got up and milled around. Break time. I headed to the bathroom, then came back to the living room and cautiously approached the couch. The hair on my arms prickled, maybe from the healing energy Madóran was using.

"Amanda, please bring a glass of water," Madóran said.

"Sure."

I fetched it and came back, waiting. After a couple of minutes Madóran took his hands away from Savhoran's face and reached for the water. He handed it to Savhoran, who chugged it.

"More?" I asked.

"Yes," said Madóran.

I fetched another glass and Savhoran drank half of it in one pull, then slowed down. I sat on the floor at his feet, watching Madóran move his hands in the air over Savhoran's face, then shoulders, then chest.

"Be more cautious in future," Madóran told him.

"I was cautious—I put on this coat—"

"It would be best if you remained indoors during daylight. You are at your most vulnerable now. Your sensitivity will decrease, but only gradually."

Savhoran didn't seem to like that information. I touched his hand and he looked down at me.

"Amanda is wounded," he said to Madóran.

"I'm all right—"

"Let me see," said Madóran.

I submitted to his inspection, which consisted of holding his hand over the cut on my neck. It felt incredibly warm—not uncomfortable, but so warm it made me sleepy. I blinked when he took his hand away.

"She will be all right."

I looked up to see Madóran smiling at me. Savhoran looked doubtful. I leaned my head against Savhoran's knee, wishing there was a way to make everything better. He caressed my hair and I felt like purring.

The others came back, bringing a couple of chairs from the nook so everyone had a seat. I stayed where I was.

Lomen brought a tray with a teapot and mugs. Once we all had tea, Caeran turned to Savhoran.

"Len and Amanda are going back to Guadalupita with Madóran."

I sat up. "I haven't agreed to that."

Caeran glowered at me. "It will free us to hunt in earnest."

"Forgive me, but so far your hunting has turned up zip."

There was a frozen silence. I swallowed, wondering if I'd just pissed them all off.

I remembered something Len had told me last fall. The clan had been camping by the river when she first met them.

"What about the bosque?" I said. "Have you searched there?"

Savhoran gave me a confused look. "Bosque?"

"The cottonwood forest by the river," I said. "It runs all through town."

Caeran's eye got intense. "Where we dwelt when we arrived."

"Yeah."

"We go tonight," Caeran said. He looked as grim as I'd

ever seen him. "Madóran, how soon can you leave?"

"I have called to order a car. It should be here within the hour."

"Len, Manda, pack your things."

Shit. I wanted to stay. I wanted to be with Savhoran every moment.

He laid his hand on my head again. *You must go. We cannot hunt until you are safe.*

I closed my eyes. *Promise you won't go out in the sun.*

I won't today.

That wasn't good enough. I swallowed.

I'm worth living for, right?

His answer was wordless, and took my breath away. It was like he poured love into me. That's inadequate, but there's really no way to describe it.

I stood. "I think I can take a week off of work without getting fired. What about you, Len?"

She shrugged. "I can try."

"OK." I looked at Caeran. "You have a week."

I went to my room, pulled my bag out from under the bed, and grabbed clothes out of my dresser at random. I threw in my computer and my cell phone charger, got my toothbrush and stuff from the bathroom, then sat on the bed and indulged in a few sobs.

I was scared of the alben, yes. I wanted the clan to succeed in catching her, and if I had to get out of the way for that to happen, so be it.

So grow up, I told myself. Get a grip.

I went back to the bathroom and washed my face. Got the bandage wet so I pulled it off, intending to replace it. Then I stared in the mirror.

The cut was gone. Not just closed, *gone*. Not even a scar. I rubbed where it had been, and the skin there was a little sensitive, but that was all.

So OK, Madóran was not just a curandero, he was magic. And Len was his apprentice? Was she learning to do that?

The house was quiet when I brought my bag out to the living room. It was empty except for Savhoran sitting on the couch, frowning at the floor. He got up and came to me, smiling his sad smile.

"Where are the others?" I asked.

"Three have gone to scout the neighborhood. Madóran is calling Nathrin and Mirali. And Caeran and Len are saying goodbye."

I swallowed. *No giving up, OK?*

You will see me again.

Soon?

I hope so.

He gathered me into his arms and just held me for a while. I was fighting not to cry again. He kissed my temple and I closed my eyes. He'd found the way to distract me; I turned my face toward him and was rewarded with a serious kiss.

It is amazing to be kissed by someone whose feelings you can feel, and vice versa. It's this incredible—I guess they call it a feedback loop? Anyway, just astounding. I wanted to drag him back to my bedroom for more.

The front door opened. Savhoran kissed my forehead and let me go.

Madóran came in, cell phone in hand. Seeing him reminded me of my healed cut. I glanced up at Savhoran and saw that his face was better, too—a little pink, but not the lobster-like color he'd been when he came in. I just gazed at him, trying to memorize his face, so beautiful and so sad.

He must have heard that, because he looked at me and smiled. *Not always sad.*

I wish I could make you happy.

You do.

Caeran and Len came out of their bedroom, Caeran carrying her bag. Len was kind of hanging on his arm.

"The car is here," Madóran said. "We will stop at the hotel to pick up Nathrin and Mirali. I will call from there to let you know we are leaving."

Caeran nodded. "Thank you. We continue to be in your debt."

Madóran shook his head, smiling. "I am happy to have company."

Savhoran reached for my bag.

"No!" Madóran and I said together.

"The sun is still up," Madóran said, taking the bag from him.

Savhoran's jaw tightened. I hugged him as Caeran and Len followed Madóran out.

Don't forget me, OK?

Never. You are all I have.

That's not true! You have the clan!

But they fear me, and rightly so. I cannot be close to my own kind any more.

And that grief overwhelmed all his other sorrows. I wiped at my face, not wanting to give him a weepy farewell.

They still love you. And so do I.

He hugged me so hard it almost hurt, then let me go and kissed me lightly.

They are waiting.

I didn't want to go. *Will you be able to talk to me like this?*

Probably not over distance. That is a rare gift. And even if I could, I would not want to while we are hunting. It would be too distracting.

Oh. Yeah, I can see that.

Now go, Amanda. This is hard for me, too.

I went to the door and looked back. *Call me, OK? When you're not busy hunting?*

All right.

I made myself go out into the sunlight that was now an enemy. Caeran nodded at me as we passed on the walk. His face looked strained.

A beige minivan sat at the curb, not looking like a limo. The driver who opened the door for me was an ordinary human, which meant we wouldn't be able to talk about stuff in the car. I got in next to Len in the back seat and stared at the house.

Caeran was standing on the front porch. I looked toward the curtained living room window. Savhoran was there—I couldn't see him but I knew it. I felt him watching as the van pulled away. I missed him already.

~

The drive was long and boring. Len apparently didn't feel like talking any more than I did. I stared out the window and thought about Savhoran. We picked up Nathrin and Mirali at a hotel, stopped a couple of times for gas and bathroom breaks, and arrived in Guadalupita about an hour after dark.

My heart was aching, but I couldn't help being glad to be back in that beautiful place. Crickets chirped and the stars glowed overhead while the driver put our bags on the *portal*. I stared up at the sky, thinking about Savhoran. The van drove away, its noise fading for a long time until all I could hear were the crickets.

The clan must be hunting now. I swallowed, wished them luck, then followed the others inside.

They were talking in the entryway. Madóran turned as I came in. "Dinner will be ready in a short while," he said. "You will have your usual rooms."

He headed toward the kitchen, leaving us to settle in on our own. Len picked up her bag and opened the door to the *plazuela*. I followed and went to my former room, which had been made up fresh. I put my bag on the floor and flopped onto the bed. I must have been tired, or maybe just stressed. I fell asleep.

A knocking on my door woke me. I sat up, slowly figuring out where I was.

"Hey, Man—you in there?" Len's voice.

"Uh-huh," I said, still groggy.

"Come on, dinner's ready."

The second I opened the door the smell of Madóran's cooking got me. My stomach growled as I followed Len across the courtyard.

Mirali and Nathrin were already at the table, talking in ælven with Madóran who was at the stove. They switched to English when we came in. I gathered they were going to stay at the house for now; Nathrin said something about going to get their clothes in the morning. They had been staying somewhere else nearby the first time I came, but now with the alben running around I guess they wanted more security.

Madóran had made steak, potatoes, and asparagus with lemon sauce. I forced myself not to gobble, to slow down and savor everything.

Len picked at her food. Missing Caeran, I figured. I didn't want to get depressed, so I listened to the ælven as a distraction.

"I will take the first watch tonight," Madóran said to Nathrin. "I will call you after midnight."

"How can I help?" I asked. "I could take a turn."

Nathrin looked at me. "You need to sleep."

"Well, so do you guys, right?"

He looked amused and glanced at Madóran, who handed him the asparagus.

"We do not sleep, Amanda," Madóran said. "Not as you do. Our bodies require rest, but not sleep."

"It's more like meditation," Len put in.

I looked at her. "So Caeran meditates while you sleep? What does he do when you snore?"

She frowned at me, then cut a bite of her steak. "If I'm restless he goes somewhere else to rest. But he really only needs about four hours a day."

"Jeez."

I ate a bite of potato, feeling inferior. Why did the ælven bother with us at all? Probably they didn't want to, but we were more populous so they had to deal with us or hide in the middle of nowhere.

It occurred to me to wonder if the ælven were approaching extinction. I looked at Madóran and he gave me a sad smile.

Crap. That shouldn't happen. They were so amazing. And they were here before us—somebody'd said that, probably Caeran.

Deep inside me something stirred. If there was anything I could do to help the ælven, I wanted to. Trouble was, I didn't know how. Following in Len's footsteps didn't feel like enough, and I was pretty sure I couldn't improve on what she was doing.

I envied her a little. She had figured out what she could do. If she and Madóran really found a cure, then maybe all the alben could reunite with the ælven, and there'd be more of them, and they wouldn't go extinct.

And if she found a cure, maybe Savhoran would get better. My heart clenched at that. It was almost enough to make me change my mind about studying medicine.

Nathrin and Mirali went to their room after dinner. Len and I did the dishes while Madóran put away leftovers. I continued to mull over what I could do to help.

"What are you good at?" Madóran asked.

"Huh?"

"Do you have skills, or pastimes you enjoy?"

"Um. Poker. Playing video games and watching movies. That's probably not what you meant."

"You never know when something may be of use. What are the video games that you enjoy like?"

"Puzzles, mostly. I'm not much into shoot-em-ups."

Madóran looked confused.

"Violent stuff," I added.

"Ah."

I was tired, and Len looked sleepy. When the kitchen was squared away we called it a night. Madóran came with us to the courtyard and said goodnight there. I went to my room, and glanced back at the door.

Madóran was sitting in a chair near the fountain, staring up at the sky. It didn't look like he was keeping watch, but I knew he was, and that was really reassuring. I went to bed and slept like a log.

The next morning I had to look at my phone to remember what day it was. Friday, right. I had to call in sick. I decided I needed breakfast before facing that.

I got dressed and headed across the courtyard, drawn by the smell of cinnamon. Madóran had made sticky buns and they were heaven. He smiled at me from the counter where he was cutting up oranges.

Len was at the table ahead of me; no sign of Nathrin or Mirali. I sat across from Len and poured myself some tea.

"Did you call in?" Len asked.

"I will. You?"

"Yeah. Alice wasn't pleased when I said I was taking a week off."

"Did you tell her it was an emergency?"

"I said family business. Didn't impress her."

She seemed a little down, so I changed the subject. "Have you talked to Caeran?"

"Yeah. You were right. They found where the alben had

been camping in the bosque. She wasn't there, though. They staked it out all night, but she didn't come back."

Now I was depressed. I ate three sticky buns, drank some tea, and ate a couple of orange slices for virtue's sake, then went out to the *plazuela* to call the library.

Dave was in. I took a deep breath and told him I was taking the next week off. He was usually a jerk about changes to the schedule, but Poppy must have given him a full dramatic reenactment of my adventure in the ladies' room, because he didn't say a thing except that he hoped I would feel better soon.

I said goodbye and then stared at my phone a while, wondering whether to call Savhoran. He had said he would call, and if he was resting after hunting all night I didn't want to bother him. I decided to wait and if he didn't call by the next morning, I'd call him.

I stared at the courtyard. Bees and butterflies were visiting the flowers. A robin was taking a bath in the fountain, splashing water everywhere, having a grand time.

Len came out and sat in the chair next to mine. "So, here we are."

"Yeah."

I looked up at the sky—deep blue up here away from city smog. Oddly, that made me homesick for Albuquerque.

"Wish we could do something to help," I said.

"We're helping by staying out of the way." She didn't sound so happy about it.

"I mean something constructive. I wish I'd taken martial arts."

Len shook her head. "Wouldn't work. She can control you."

I shivered, remembering. "She can't do that to ælven, can she? Just to us?"

"Right. We're weaker, easier to control. She can do it to

ælven, but not as well, and only one at a time."

"Pepper spray! I meant to say they should all carry it, but I forgot. I couldn't use mine, but if Lomen had had one—will you tell Caeran?"

"Yeah. Good idea."

Movement caught my eye: Nathrin came out of a door on the west side of the house and walked along the *portal* to the kitchen. He nodded when he saw me watching, but didn't stop. When he'd gone inside I turned to Len.

"Is Caeran afraid of Savhoran?"

"Afraid? No. He's sad for him."

"Savhoran thinks they're all afraid of him."

"They're afraid of the disease. Mirali most of all, I think. Can't blame her."

"No...but he misses them." I sighed. "I wish there was something I could do."

Len grinned. "I could think of a few things."

"Yeah, great. Except I'm two hundred miles away."

Nathrin came out of the kitchen with a tray of food and tea, and went back down the *portal*. Mirali was getting breakfast in bed, I guessed.

"Mirali doesn't like me," I said.

"She's not that wild about humans in general, especially when they hook up with members of her clan."

"So she's a bigot?"

Len shrugged. "She's seen her friends break their hearts over humans more than once. She tried to talk me out of being with Caeran. Told me about the last time he got involved with a human. It was pretty sad; I almost gave him up."

"Crap! No!"

"Yeah. But Caeran had other ideas." She smiled softly. "We're lucky, you know, you and I."

"I know."

Even though Savhoran suffered this disease—or maybe because of it—I was lucky. He wanted me, even needed me. It still amazed me when I thought about it that he should care about me at all. I mean, we must seem like fruit flies to them. Here today, gone tomorrow. Not even worth remembering a name.

I sat up, trying to shake myself out of moping. "Guess I'll get my book."

Len got hers, too—a fat medical book that she'd borrowed from the library—and we spent the morning reading. Madóran called us in for lunch. I asked if he needed help in the garden.

"I am done for today, but thank you. Please enjoy yourself."

"Well, I'm available for chores."

"I will bear that in mind."

He sent us back to the courtyard with a pitcher of iced lemonade. I finished the book I'd brought and bought another one on my phone. Read until I was cross-eyed, then wandered around the hacienda looking for a television. I suffered a pang of withdrawal when I realized Madóran didn't have one.

Savhoran called me that evening, a little before sundown. We had just finished supper and Len and I were lazing around on the *plazuela*. Len looked at me when my phone rang, and grinned when I headed for my room. I was blushing.

"Hi!" I said when I'd reached the *portal*. "I'm so glad you called!"

"Hello, Amanda. I wish I had good news, but I do not. We have not caught the alben."

"It's great just to hear your voice."

We talked for a while about pretty trivial stuff. It was the contact that mattered.

Over the next few days we got in the habit of talking every day, usually after suppertime.

The alben-hunting wasn't going so well. I had thought at first that the clan guys just weren't trying that hard, but after listening to Savhoran describe what they were doing at night, I changed my mind.

They combed the campus and the bosque every night. Everyone but Savhoran was hunting in the daytime as well. They watched where the alben had camped—near where the ælven's first camp had been; Len told me she'd seen it and described to me where it was, south of the nature center. That kind of creeped me out, because a lot of people use the paths along the river for biking, walking, or jogging. Easy pickings.

After three nights of staking out the bosque without success, the ælven decided to pretend that Len and I were back and they were guarding us again. It meant that two of them, Caeran and one other, had to spend days outside the lab and the library. Really tedious, and frustrating for Savhoran because he couldn't help.

We talked a little about his condition, about how hard it was for him, especially the drinking blood part. I told him it was OK if he wanted to talk to me about it some more, that I wouldn't be freaked out. But he seemed to want to avoid the subject.

My phone call with Savhoran was the best part of every day. Madóran was a considerate and generous host, and I fell in love with his house, but it wasn't home. I felt like my life was on hold.

July arrived, but the monsoons hadn't started yet. It was the time of year when New Mexicans hoped and prayed for the summer rains to come.

Madóran's garden was now bursting with squash and beans and tomatoes. I helped him work there in the mornings, sat on my lazy ass and read in the afternoons, and in the evenings we all hung out in the living room and played games or made music. If it was music I let the others do the making. Every artist needs an audience.

We saw Mirali occasionally at meals, Nathrin more often. Sometimes they'd join us in the evening, but mostly it was just us three.

By Friday the clan still hadn't caught the alben, and Len and I had to call in and tell our bosses we needed another week off. Dave wasn't in (yes, I called ten minutes before he usually arrived) so I left a message.

Len didn't get off so easy. Her boss kind of raked her over the coals. She was bummed about it, and predicted that she would lose the job.

That evening I taught Madóran how to play poker. He liked games, and had taught us some ælven games played with polished stones on a decorated cloth. Card games were fairly new for him—he'd never played until Christmastime, when Len had brought a deck up with her and taught him and Caeran to play spades.

We used Madóran's polished stones for poker chips. He caught on scary fast, and after moving from draw to stud, I suggested we play Texas Hold'em.

"That's not fair," Len said. "The odds are all different."

"You watch. He'll be beating us in less than an hour."

He did. He took all our stones in probably less than half an hour.

"I like this game," Madóran said. "Let us play again!"

Len glared at him. "OK, fine, but I need caffeine."

"I will make some tea—"

"No, I'll get it," she said, standing up. "You guys relax."

Left alone with Madóran, I gave him a smile. "I can't believe you never played poker before. I mean, this was the wild west, and you were here."

"I have always been rather isolated. Entirely by choice, of

course. I believe I may have been invited to play poker, but did not accept." He gathered the stones and began sorting them by color: green, blue, and white.

I shuffled the cards. "Well if you ever needed money, you could probably win at a casino."

He smiled, but didn't answer. I suspected he had no need for extra money, or if he did he had ways of getting it that he preferred to going out amidst throngs of gambling humans. He was a genuine recluse, and I reminded myself that he was honoring us by letting us stay with him.

I pondered that. The ælven seemed to have no shortage of money. What they needed, as Len had said, was access to a lab for research. And the skills to use it, which was why Len was in med school.

Could they create their own private lab? Or would that cost too much even for them? I suspected there were fancy, expensive machines involved. Electron microscopes and things. Even Madóran might not be able to afford that.

I looked out the window and saw someone standing outside. Caught my breath in fear, then the next moment I felt a rush of attraction to the man standing in front of the house.

It was late, but there was moonlight, enough to gleam off of snow white hair.

= 9 =

I stood and went over to the window. Was it Savhoran? That question should have mattered more than it did.

Whoever it was, he was gorgeous. I knew it, even though I only saw glimpses of his face: the line of a cheekbone, the pale brow. I wanted to go out to him, because he was already making me feel wonderful and I knew it would only get better.

A tiny part of my mind protested this. That small part was loyal to Savhoran, and made me feel something was wrong.

I drew a sharp breath. "Madóran!"

It was a whisper, but he came over at once, and when he looked out the window he hissed. He pulled the curtain across the window in front of me, then put his hand on my shoulder. I felt the warmth of it melt through me, and my mind cleared. Suddenly I was afraid.

"Stay here," he said, and went out through the entryway.

The front door closed. I stumbled over to the couch, confused.

I heard voices, Madóran's and the stranger's, talking in ælven. I felt shaky and wanted to call Savhoran, but it was night and he would be hunting.

Gradually I came to realize that I'd been controlled again, just in a different way. A terrifying way. Someone—Caeran? —had said that alben liked to go after the opposite sex, using seduction to disarm their victims. I had thought normal seduction. This was something else.

Len came back with a tea tray which she set on the coffee

table. "Where's Madóran?"

"Outside. Talking to—to an alben."

"*What!?*"

She started toward the window. I got in front of her.

"Don't look! He did a whammy on me just through the window."

She looked alarmed at that. "He? It's not the same one?"

I shook my head. "Madóran said to stay inside."

"But he's alone out there! Defenseless!"

"They're just talking. And anyway, what could we do?"

She got a grim look on her face and pulled her pepper spray out of her pocket. I hadn't expected her to keep carrying it here—mine was in my room—and I wondered what had made her so paranoid. Sadly, it wasn't misplaced.

She went to the window and peeked around the edge of the curtain. "You're right, they're just talking. Oh, jeez!"

She turned away from the window and stood blinking. I went over to her and touched her arm.

"You OK?"

She closed her eyes and drew a deep breath. "Yeah. He looked at me. Damn it! Gehmanin didn't do that!"

"Who?"

She met my gaze. "The campus killer from last fall."

"Oh."

"He never did that mesmerizing thing to me. He was always just angry. No wonder Caeran's afraid of the female!"

"Why should he be afraid? She's after humans, not ælven."

"She can feed on ælven, too. Humans are just easier to control. The other thing is that she may want to breed."

"Oh! Holy crap!"

"Yeah."

Len sat on the couch and glanced toward the window. They were still talking outside, so I guessed Madóran was all right, but I didn't like it. Neither did Len.

She stood up. "I'm going to get Nathrin."

I watched her go out through the entryway to the *plazuela*. Thought about getting my pepper spray from my room, but before I could do it I heard the front door.

I waited, holding my breath, hoping the alben hadn't come inside. When Madóran came in alone I sighed with relief.

"He is gone," Madóran said.

"For good?"

"I hope so. I asked him to hunt elsewhere."

"You mean you can just ask an alben to do something and they will?"

"It depends on the alben."

Madóran pulled the curtains over all the windows, then sat on the couch and poured tea. He offered me a mug. My hand shook a little as I took it.

"Where is Len?" he asked.

"She went to tell Nathrin."

Even as I said it, the entry door opened and they both came in. Nathrin looked ready for a fight.

"Where is he?"

"Gone," Madóran said.

Nathrin's eyes narrowed. "You are certain?"

Madóran gave a small shrug. "Not absolutely. I asked him to leave and he agreed, but he could return."

Nathrin pressed his lips together. "Who was it?"

"Pirian."

Frowning, Nathrin took two steps backward, then turned and left. Going back to protect his lady.

Len came and sat next to me. Madóran gave her a mug of tea.

"So it was someone you know?" I asked.

He nodded. "An old acquaintance. Gehmanin told Pirian

that he was coming to look for me, and Pirian decided to follow."

Len didn't look happy about that.

"Why?" I asked.

Madóran sighed. "They were lovers. Pirian contracted the disease from Gehmanin. He was … jealous."

I frowned, not getting it. "Jealous of you?"

He nodded, then put his face in his hands. Len shot me a warning glance, so I quit asking questions.

"If there's anything we can do to help, please tell us," she said.

He looked up at her, then at me. "Do not go outside alone. It would be best if you did not go out without me."

"But the *plazuela*'s OK, right?" I asked.

Madóran shook his head slowly. "Not really."

Len looked at me. "He can climb. Heck, with a step up, I could climb onto the roof of the *portal*, and any ælven is way more agile than me."

I was used to thinking the hacienda was like a fortress. Trouble was, it was built to protect against human enemies, not ælven. It was defensible, yes, but that took defenders. There were three of us—five if you counted Nathrin and Mirali—and I was pretty sure that wasn't enough.

"We must stay together," Madóran said. "Amanda, I think it would be best if you moved in with Len. Her room is next to mine, and Nathrin and Mirali are in the chamber on the other side."

"Should I call Caeran?" Len asked.

Madóran frowned. "I think … yes. We must ask them to come."

"And Savhoran, right?" I said.

He looked pained. "Savhoran is vulnerable. It might be better..."

"If they left him alone in Albuquerque?" I said. "I don't

think so."

"There is no good solution." Madóran sighed. "Please tell him he is welcome to come. The choice is his."

I nodded and took out my cell phone. Len was already texting on hers. Savhoran didn't know how to text yet, so I called his number and wandered over toward the dining table at the far end of the room. I felt Madóran watching me.

I got Savhoran's voicemail. Probably he'd left the phone at home while he went out hunting with the others. I left a message asking him to call me, then put my phone away and went back to the couch.

My tea was lukewarm. I drank it anyway; black tea with mint to soothe the nerves. I was picking up a little herbal knowledge from Madóran, for whatever good it would do me. Not much if I didn't survive the summer.

"They're in the bosque," Len said. "Caeran's going to gather the others."

"Is Savhoran with them?" I asked.

"He didn't say."

We finished our tea, then Madóran led us around the house, locking all the doors and windows. We went around the *plazeula*, too, closing the doors in the glass wall. I hadn't noticed, but they all had bolt latches. Not that that would do a lot; anyone determined to get in could simply break the glass.

Madóran held his hand on each doorknob and murmured something. I thought I saw a glow of light under his hand, and I definitely felt the back of my neck prickling.

When everything was as secure as it would get, Madóran made me pack up my stuff and he and Len helped me move it to her room. I'd probably get moved again when Caeran and the others got here, but for now I was glad not to be alone.

Len's room was in the middle of the hacienda's west side,

and the curtains and all the bedding were deep blue, while the lamps had mica shades that glowed orange-gold. There was a dresser that looked at least a hundred years old. On top of it was a wooden tray carved with mermaids. Too gorgeous for its current contents, which had last resided in Len's pockets. Handful of change, keychain, lip gloss.

Besides the bedroom furniture, every inch of available wall space was filled with bookcases. There was only one bed but it was huge, so Len and I wouldn't be getting in each other's way. Over the headboard hung a Georgia O'Keeffe painting; an original, I suspected. There was another over the dresser.

Madóran went to a door in the room's south wall and undid the latch hook. "This leads to my sitting room. The opposite door leads to Nathrin and Mirali's room. We must leave them all unlatched, so that we can move among these rooms without going onto the *portal* if need be."

Len nodded. "What about meals?"

"I will prepare a store of food that we can keep here, enough for a few days. I hope we shall not have to use it. Meanwhile, we should all move to and from the public rooms together."

Madóran went to the east door, the one that opened on the *plazuela*. "I will tell Nathrin and Mirali this plan. Please do not go out."

He left, closing the door gently behind him. Len and I looked at each other.

"Let me clear a couple of drawers for you," she said, heading for the dresser.

"Don't bother. Caeran will be here soon. I'll just live out of my bag."

She sat on the bed, sighing. "I'm sorry about all this."

"It's not your fault."

"I feel like it is."

"Don't." I sat next to her. "Listen, the minute Savhoran came into the picture, I stayed because I wanted to. You're not responsible."

Len smiled sadly. "I'm glad you like him. He was so crushed when Tiruli left."

"Tiruli? Was that...?"

"His partner. *Ex*-partner. She just couldn't handle it. I guess I understand why, but she really let him down right when he needed support."

"Did they do that—that thing you and Caeran did at Midsummer?"

"Cup-bond. Yeah, they were supposed to renew it at Evennight, but Tiruli left before then."

"Evennight?"

"The equinox. Spring, in this case. Savhoran didn't celebrate it with the others, just stayed holed up in his room. I was afraid he'd—well, give up."

"Suicide."

She nodded.

"He still might." I swallowed; I hadn't voiced that fear before. "He's having a hard time with this disease."

"He's doing a lot better since he met you."

"Thanks."

That gave me a little warm glow in my belly. Len hugged me, then we got ready for bed. Madóran came back through the door to Nathrin and Mirali's room, told us to come use his bathroom if we needed to, then said good night.

Maybe from stress, or from being in a new room, I had trouble getting to sleep. When I finally did drop off, I dreamed about the alben guy. Just like the reality had been, the dream was exciting and horrifying at the same time, only this time there was no Madóran to intervene, so the alben got to me and, well, let's just say it would probably be a hit at the movies. But I didn't like it. Enjoyed; didn't like.

I figured out that it was a dream and struggled to wake up. Finally succeeded and opened my eyes. The room was very still and dark. I looked around, then froze.

I could just see the silhouette of a man standing at the foot of the bed.

I sat up, fixing to scream.

Don't be afraid. It's me.

Relief washed through me, along with a breathtaking awareness of Caeran. He'd never talked to me like that before. It reassured me that all my ideas about him were correct.

Did you just get here?

Yes. I didn't know you were sharing Len's room.

Madóran wanted us all together. I moved to get out of the bed.

No, stay there. Don't wake her.

Caeran went and sat in the armchair across the room. I couldn't see his face.

How did you get in? We locked everything up—

Madóran gave me a key last winter.

Oh. I hesitated, then figured what the hell. He could probably tell what I was thinking anyway. *Where's Savhoran?*

I sensed a flicker of frustration, then Caeran tightened his shielding. Duh—I'd forgotten. I hastily put some white light around myself.

He wouldn't come. He didn't want to make the others uncomfortable.

Five was a tight fit in Len's car, but I suspected that wasn't the reason. Savhoran was sensitive; he knew the rest of the clan didn't like being physically close to him.

So he's alone?

I offered to go back for him, but he didn't want me to take the risk.

I was not happy about this. I concentrated on the white

light for a minute, not wanting my feelings to annoy Caeran.

I called his cell, but he didn't answer.

He may have left it at home.

Yeah, probably. Crap.

In a day or two, if things are quiet here, I will go back for him.

Thanks.

Rest, now. I must talk to Madóran.

OK. I'm glad you're here.

His answer was wordless and warm. He went to the door into Madóran's room, and by the time he closed it, he'd slipped out of contact.

I sighed. I was glad Caeran and the others had come, but I was worried about Savhoran. It was hard to keep from grabbing my phone and calling again right then, but there was no point in doing that before morning. I lay down and kept my thoughts firmly on Savhoran until I fell asleep.

Len tickled me awake. I sat up gasping and thrashing.

She laughed. Daylight was streaming in behind her through a window to the *portal*.

"Dammit!" I aimed a pillow at her. She dodged so it just hit a glancing blow.

She grinned. "Get up, lazy. Breakfast is ready."

I slithered to my feet and pulled my t-shirt down. "You just want me out of your bed now that Caeran's back."

"How did you know he was back?"

"Um. He stopped by. You were asleep."

"Oh." She looked momentarily unhappy, then dismissed it. "Come on, before they eat all the waffles."

I pulled on my jeans and combed my hair with my fingers as we went out to the *portal*. Apparently it was OK to walk around out there during daylight, but the glass doors were all still latched. Out in the *plazuela* a breeze stirred the roses and bees hummed around the pansies.

The kitchen was full of ælven and smelled like maple

syrup and sausage. My stomach informed me the menu was acceptable. Len went to sit by Caeran, so I went over to the counter and put some sausage and sliced melon on a plate.

Madóran was pouring batter into an old-fashioned cast iron waffler on the stove. He closed it, then smiled at me. "Good morning."

I swallowed a bite of melon. "Morning. Smells fantastic."

"This one will be yours. The others have all had at least one."

I poured myself some tea and stood leaning against the counter, since the chairs were all taken. Nathrin and Mirali were over on the banco by the fireplace with plates in their laps. Caeran, Len, and the other three were at the table. There would have been room for everyone at the big table in the great room, but it was cozier in the kitchen, and the closeness felt safer.

The whole clan—at least the New Mexico branch, there might be others—was assembled. Savhoran should have been there, too.

I pushed that thought away and munched on a sausage until my waffle was ready. I slathered it with butter and drenched it with maple syrup—the real stuff—and stood at the counter eating while I watched Madóran make the next one.

"Would you like another?"

"In a bit. I want to call Savhoran."

"I tried," Caeran said from the table. "He's still not answering."

"Well, then I'll leave him a message."

I was in a stubborn mood. I started for the door to the *portal*, and Lomen got up and followed me. I was about to tell him to mind his own business, but Madóran caught my eye.

"Do not go outside alone, even in daylight."

I swallowed my cranky response and looked at Lomen.

"Thanks."

He smiled and walked with me to Len's room. I got out my phone and noticed it was nearly dead. Called Savhoran's number and listened to it ring, then fought back tears as the voicemail kicked in.

"Hi, Savhoran, it's Manda. Give me a call please."

That's all I said, because my voice was pretty shaky. I hung up, dug out my charger, plugged it in, and stuck the phone in it.

"Do not worry," Lomen said as we walked back to the kitchen. "Savhoran may have forgotten to charge his phone. He has done so before. Your technology is difficult for us."

"You guys have been here for like six months, right?"

"Yes, but we have not been using phones that long. Caeran got his at Evennight—it was a gift from Len—and Savhoran only got his a few weeks ago."

I stopped, trying to get the better of my dread. "Where is he if he isn't at home?"

Lomen met my gaze and I felt his sympathy. "I do not know, but he is alive. We would know if he had crossed."

I blinked. "You're all that connected?"

He nodded. "So be at ease. He is well."

As well as he could be.

Madóran was still making waffles. I'd lost my appetite, so I got a mug of tea and sat on the banco nursing it. Nathrin and Mirali were talking in ælven on the other side of the fireplace.

I felt like an outsider, honorary clan membership notwithstanding. My heart was back in Albuquerque with Savhoran. He was an outcast too, sort of. They could say all they wanted that he was still family, but he knew the difference, and so did I.

I thought about taking Len's car to go find him, but I knew what wouldn't go over well. Madóran wanted me to stay at the hacienda, and he was probably right that I was safer there than anywhere else.

So. Wait it out. Not fun.

At the table they were talking strategy now, so I drifted over to listen. Bironan wanted to go pro-active and hunt the alben down, but Faranin was arguing for caution.

"There are two of them now."

"And six of us," said Bironan, glancing over his shoulder at Nathrin. "We should be able to overcome them, even if they band together."

"But Mirali—and the mortals—must be protected."

"So the most effective use of our strength is to let them come to us," said Lomen.

"Yes," said Faranin.

"If we hunt them separately, three of us should be enough to take them," Bironan argued. "Let Nathrin, Madóran, and Caeran stay here."

"Pirian did us no harm," said Madóran, his face troubled. "I asked him to leave and he did."

"Then we hunt the other, the female."

"You do not know where she is," said Madóran. "You could exhaust yourselves searching."

"Have there been no more human victims?"

Len took out her phone and surfed up some news. She glanced up at me. "Another killing on campus two nights ago. Looks like our girl's still in town."

"Who was it?" I asked.

"No one we know."

Our gazes held. I swallowed. We both knew it could have been one of us.

"So we three return to the city," Bironan said. "With Savhoran to help us, we will be four."

No one pointed out that five of them had been hunting the alben for weeks without success. She must have found a really good hiding place. I wondered idly if the coffin full of dirt was one of the myths that was true. Couldn't really picture the alben—either of them—bedding down like that.

A thought occurred to me. I didn't like it, but I ought to bring it up.

"What if more of them come?" I asked.

They all stared at me. They didn't like the idea either.

"More alben," I added. "The latest one came looking for Madóran, right?"

Faranin turned to Madóran. "Will others seek you?"

Madóran gave a helpless shrug.

"Pirian is a greater danger in that respect. He might tell others where you are."

Madóran's eyes flashed. "And so you would kill him? No, Faranin. I will not have that on my conscience."

"We must act now," said Bironan. "Hunt the female down, then return here. I will go."

Lomen looked from him to Faranin. "I think we should."

"How will you get there?" I asked. "Do any of you drive?"

Lomen looked at me, slightly amused. "We are used to traveling on foot."

"But that'll take days! Won't it? Look, I could drive you guys. I'd be safe with four of you."

Len frowned. "Manda—"

"And Savhoran can look after me while you're hunting."

"He will not agree to that," said Lomen. "He has claimed the kill."

They were all quiet, and I knew they wouldn't let me go. I went to the counter and poured myself more tea, trying to collect myself.

"Let us make no decision as yet," said Madóran. "Bironan, I understand your desire for haste, but let us think on this a day."

Bironan bit his lip but didn't disagree. Faranin nodded. Lomen stood and murmured something to Bironan, and the two of them went out. End of discussion, for now.

I wondered who was the leader here. Faranin was the oldest, or one of the oldest. But even he deferred to Madóran. They all did. I'd assume he was the leader, except he wasn't a member of the clan.

I gave up thinking about it. I didn't understand the ælven in a lot of ways.

Nathrin and Mirali passed me on their way to their room. Nathrin glanced at me and smiled. They'd been listening; they knew the problem. Probably they'd rather have the whole clan stay here, to help protect Mirali.

Faranin followed them out. Len and Caeran brought their dishes to the counter and then left, leaving just me and Madóran.

Guess that was my cue. I turned to the sink and looked for dish soap.

"You need not do that."

"You made a great breakfast, least I can do is help clean up."

He let me wash dishes while he put stuff away, then he dried the clean plates. It went pretty fast. When everything was done, he made another pot of tea and carried it to the table, beckoning me to join him.

I sat across from him and wrapped my hands around my mug, enjoying the warmth. Outside in the courtyard birds were quarreling. I wanted to be out there, and knowing I couldn't put a gloom over me. It felt like we were under siege.

I looked at Madóran, who was musing. "You've been here a long time. Have other alben found you before? Before last fall, I mean."

He let out a slow breath. "No. A few ælven have come

across me in their travels, but no alben until now."

"Something's going to have to change."

His brow creased. "You are right."

I sipped my tea. "Len said you came with the Spanish colonists. Have you always lived in this house?"

He smiled. "Ever since I built it."

"You built it?"

"I had help. I had to learn how to make the adobe bricks. This was the first room."

I looked around the kitchen, picturing Madóran building it brick by brick, in the hot sun. "Wow. The fireplace, too?"

"No. A kiva fireplace is tricky to build. I had a master fireplace builder make that one, and two of the others. He let me help, and I learned enough to do a passable job on the rest of the house as I added rooms. It is larger than I need—usually—but I liked the hacienda style. I visited some wealthy patients in their homes, and decided to make mine in the same way. I like the private garden, especially."

I nodded, looking out the window. "Yours is beautiful."

"Thank you. I am sorry you cannot enjoy it just now, but this will pass."

"So what do we do? Wait until they catch the female, then what? Do you trust Pirian?"

He looked troubled. "No, but I do not think he is interested in hunting you and Len, particularly. I told him you were my guests, and asked him to hunt elsewhere. I hope he will honor that."

"Did you tell him about the cure?"

Madóran shook his head. "The cure is only a dream for now. I cannot placate the alben with a dream."

"You don't think it would give them hope?"

"To raise that hope without being certain we can fulfill it would be cruel."

He drank some tea. I watched him, thinking how

amazing he was. If I hadn't fallen for Savhoran I'd have fallen for him.

"How can I help?"

He looked up at me with a quick smile. "You are helping. Len misses her own kind when she is with us. Your company is good for her."

"Thanks, but that's not what I meant. I was thinking about the cure."

"Are you interested in studying medicine?"

"Not really. Len's been bugging me to take classes with her."

"The more souls we have working on the project, the better our chance of success."

I stared at my cup. "Does Savhoran know about the cure?"

"Yes. He is very important to the effort. We need the cooperation of someone afflicted with the curse, so that we can test our findings."

"And he agreed to that?"

He nodded. "I admit that one of my reasons for asking him now, even though we will have no need of him for some years, was a desire to keep him from taking his life."

And was that cruel? To save his life with a hope that might not pan out?

My eyes started to sting. I drank the last of my tea, trying to steady myself. Madóran laid his hand on my arm.

"You are a great blessing to him. For that alone, we honor you."

"The others are all afraid of him," I said.

"They fear the curse."

"But it doesn't bother you. I mean, you don't—shun him, I guess—like the rest of them."

"Oh, it bothers me. But Savhoran is not at fault, and his intentions are pure. I trust him. So does Caeran."

"Yeah. Caeran is cool."

Madóran filled both our mugs. "You are thinking, perhaps, of Mirali. She has every reason to avoid Savhoran. We do not know exactly how the disease is transmitted, though the more intimate the contact the more likely it will pass. I had thought that any attack would cause infection, but Caeran has not succumbed. His wound was less severe than Savhoran's, but it was a bite wound."

I sucked a sharp breath. So much for no biting. "I didn't know that."

He gave a small shrug. "It is past. No sense in dwelling on it."

"How did it happen?"

"Len did not tell you?"

I shook my head. Madóran sipped his tea.

"Gehmanin—the alben who came to New Mexico last fall —abducted Len and forced her to drive him north. He wanted her to bring him here, but her car ran out of fuel. Caeran was hiding in the trunk, and came out to protect Len. He and Gehmanin fought, and he was bitten. And it was Gehmanin who later injured Savhoran."

"And you knew him."

Madóran closed his eyes. "Long ago I knew him well."

Oh, boy. I had a guess about how well.

"You're sad he's dead."

"I am sad that he was afflicted. It brought out the worst in him."

"I'm sorry."

He gave me a small smile. "Thank you. I cannot let the others see it, but I still grieve for him."

I had an urge to hug him, but I chickened out. I took another swallow of tea.

"You like guys, huh?"

His smile widened. "I like everyone."

"Oh." A tingle went through me.

He held my gaze for a moment that stretched to forever, then looked away and stood up. "I could use some help in the garden, if you are willing."

"Sure." I gulped the last of my tea and put my mug in the sink. "Um, I should move my stuff, too, now that Caeran's here."

"Ah, yes. You may put your things in your room, though if a hunting party leaves I will want you closer to the rest of us."

"OK. I'm mobile."

He walked with me to Len and Caeran's room, and while I was packing up he went two doors down to ask Lomen to come out to the garden with us. I moved to my old room, then borrowed a hat and gloves from Madóran and we grubbed in the dirt while Lomen kept watch.

I pulled weeds. It was good to do something physical and mindless. It helped dissipate the feeling of being trapped, and gave me time to do some thinking.

I really did want to help with the cure, even though I was dubious about studying medicine. Science was never my best subject. In high school my favorite classes were art and shop. I liked working with my hands, especially woodworking. Too bad building game boards wouldn't help the project.

The rest of the day I stayed inside and read. Madóran showed me his library, which was almost as big as the great room and was doubling as a guest room at the moment. There were two daybeds that folded out for sleeping, and Lomen and Bironan were crashing there.

I picked up a book that was lying on a desk by the window. It was hand-written in a beautiful script, with letters I'd never seen before though some of them looked familiar.

"That is an ælven text," Madóran said. "Len has been studying it."

"Len is learning ælven?"

"Caeran has been teaching her. She is picking it up quickly."

"Can I learn it too?"

"I imagine you could."

I turned a couple of pages. They were yellow and they crackled. "How old is this?"

"I made that copy a few decades ago. You are right, I should recopy it soon."

"You made this book."

"I made the copy. I did not write it. The author crossed centuries ago."

I shouldn't have been surprised. Madóran could do anything. He'd had a long time to learn a lot of different skills. I carefully put the book down.

Madóran gestured to a shelf. "These are the most current books I have, which is not saying much, I fear. There are a few novels from the last decade."

I picked out a book—a novel, written by a human who was probably still alive—and took it to my room, then scurried along the *portal* to Len and Caeran's room. I knocked in case they wanted to be left alone. Len came to the door.

"Madóran said you were learning ælven. Would you teach me?"

"What little I know, sure. Give me about an hour?"

"OK."

I went back to my room and read until Len knocked on my door. She was escorted by Caeran, who went with us to the great room and then went off to find Madóran. We settled in on the couch. Len had brought the ælven book from the library and a couple of notepads, one with her notes on it. She gave me the other one and a pencil and we killed a few hours going over the basics.

Ælven is as hard as it is beautiful. It doesn't have a lot in common with English, except that every now and then a word means the same thing in both languages. Len said that they were old words in English and had originally come from the ælven.

That evening we all ate supper in the great room. It felt more formal sitting around the big dining table. Dinner was roast chicken, rice, and spinach from the garden. Madóran opened a couple of bottles of wine—unlabeled, and by now I had guessed that he probably made it—and poured it for everyone but Mirali. He murmured to her in ælven and she nodded, sticking with her glass of water. They drank a toast, in ælven so I didn't understand it, but I raised my glass anyway.

The conversation was about planning ahead: specifically, whether the clan should stay in New Mexico. They talked a little about where they'd come from; somewhere in Europe, I gathered, a forest that was being invaded by humans. It sounded like they thought going back there would be even worse than dealing with the alben. I mostly listened.

When the meal was over Len and I cleared the table while the clan began to discuss the issue at hand: alben-hunting, when, where and how. They went back over the morning's argument, still disagreeing over whether they should stick together or send out a party to hunt the female. Bironan wanted to hunt, and Lomen was with him. Faranin, Nathrin, and Mirali wanted everyone to stay put. Caeran and Madóran didn't offer opinions.

It looked like they were just going to keep arguing until something happened. I got up and wandered away from the table. The front windows were still covered, so I stepped into the entryway to look out on the *plazuela*. The green smell of all the plants made me relax.

Len joined me. "This is how they work things out."

"By arguing about it over and over?"

"Yeah. It beats a war."

I shook my head, gazing out at the twilit garden. "Sometimes I don't understand them at all."

"Me neither. But it's worth it."

I glanced at her. "You think you can find a cure?"

She raised a shoulder. "I'm willing to spend my life trying."

Shouldn't I be willing, too? Savhoran needed that cure.

"I'm going to make some tea. You want anything?"

I shook my head and watched her head for the kitchen. I envied her commitment, to be honest. She knew exactly what she wanted to accomplish in this life. I didn't, really. I wanted to be with Savhoran, but that wasn't a lifetime achievement.

When she came back with a tray of teapot and mugs, I followed her back into the great room. The ælven were still debating around the dining table. Madóran smiled and nodded at Len. She and I served tea to them all, then retreated to the sofa with our own mugs. We might be honorary members of the clan, but we didn't have a say in this discussion.

To my surprise, they actually reached a decision. Bironan had worn them down and convinced them that a party should go out to hunt the female alben. Faranin finally agreed to go with him and Lomen. It sounded like they were still planning to walk.

I got up and walked over to the table. "Look, if you won't let me drive you, at least take the bus. You'll get there faster."

Bironan frowned. "Bus?"

"Yeah. You can catch one to Albuquerque from Las Vegas. Len or I could drive you there tomorrow."

"I will drive them," Caeran said.

Len whipped out her phone and surfed up the bus schedule. Plans were made, and the meeting was over.

Nathrin and Mirali headed for their room, and the rest of

them drifted over to the sofa and chairs. Madóran got out his guitar and he and Len took turns playing. On one song that Madóran played, all the ælven sang along in their language. It was so strange and beautiful it gave me goosebumps.

I got out a deck of cards and sat at the long table, playing solitaire. It helped me think.

What could I do to help? Playing poker wasn't useful, especially since money wasn't an issue.

I could boss the ælven around.

I snarked to myself as I shuffled. Probably they wouldn't put up with me telling them what to do, but I did sometimes wish I could. Their beat-the-dead-horse method of discussion was a slow way of getting things done.

Lomen came over and joined me. I dealt us a hand of Hold'em.

"We will play in another tournament," he said. "You were doing very well. You deserve another chance."

"Thanks. Your action."

"Check."

"I bet two samolians," I said.

"Call."

I dealt the flop, low mixed garbage. Lomen checked again. I looked at my cards: they hadn't changed. Jack-ten off-suited.

"Check."

Turn card: ten. Lomen checked.

"Four samolians."

He called. I turned over the river card, a seven. There was a chance of a straight. Lomen checked again.

I stared at him for a minute, trying to decide if he was slow-playing me. He gazed mildly back. Ælven don't get impatient—they have all the time in the world.

I checked and showed my hand. He turned over pocket aces.

"You should have bet those," I said.

"You would have folded."

"Maybe, but you might have won more if I called. And more to the point, I could have caught a straight and beat you. Better to bet hard with pockets."

He smiled. "I am disinclined to be aggressive. You are a better player."

In poker, yeah I guessed I was. Arrogance can pay. Not that the ælven weren't arrogant in their own way, but they were usually subtle about it.

I hastily wrapped white light around that thought. Glanced at Lomen, but he didn't show any sign of having heard.

The next morning after breakfast Caeran drove the hunting party to Las Vegas in Len's car. Still no answer when I called Savhoran's cell, and he hadn't left me a message. I tried to dismiss it, but I was worried.

I helped Madóran in the garden again, this time with Len standing guard. Nathrin was sticking close to Mirali. I missed Lomen more than I'd expected, and was glad when Caeran came back. He brought in four bags of groceries; Madóran had given him a shopping list. I helped put stuff away.

Len and I spent the rest of that day practicing ælven, with Caeran coaching us. He said I was doing well. I figured he was just being nice.

The six of us had dinner in the kitchen, and I missed the hunting party even more. There were too few of us. Dinner conversation was a bit strained, because we avoided talking about the one thing all of us were thinking about. We went our separate ways for the evening.

The next day was Monday, and Madóran had patients coming in. Len helped him, which left me to entertain myself. I left another message for Savhoran. I was tired of reading so I opened the door of my room, sat on my bed, and stared out at the *plazuela*.

Caeran walked by and noticed me sitting there. "Do you want to go outside?"

"Madóran said not to alone, even in daytime."

"I will go with you if you wish."

He didn't have to ask me twice. I went around smelling and touching every plant in the garden, I was so glad to be out there. Walked through the orchards and the vineyard. Finally I settled in a chair in the shade near the fountain, and Caeran sat next to me.

"Do you wish you were hunting too?" I asked.

He shook his head. "I wish there were no need to hunt."

"Yeah." I watched a hummingbird visit the honeysuckle vine on the south side of the *plazuela*. "What do you think that female would be like if she was cured?"

He thought for a moment. "She might be the same. She may have developed a taste for blood. Gehmanin was unimpressed at the possibility of a cure."

Oh, great.

"Do you think any of the alben will be interested? I mean, why go to the trouble if they're not?"

"For Savhoran."

"Well, yeah. But will any of the others want the cure?"

"Most will, I think. Pirian may. I wish I had been here when Madóran talked with him."

"Do you know him?"

"No."

"He hasn't been back, so I guess he kept his word."

Caeran nodded.

I sat thinking about the future, when the cure had been found and Madóran's patients were all alben coming to the hacienda to be treated. A parade of them coming in, with Len and Madóran working on them and me directing traffic. Caeran and Lomen standing watch in case one of the alben went rogue. When the patients came out of the treatment room their hair wasn't white anymore, but brown like the clan's or black like Madoran's. Each of them left a pile of gold coins or a handful of gems on my desk.

"Manda?"

Gentle voice startled me awake. I blinked, realizing it was Caeran.

"Madóran has lunch ready."

We went to the kitchen and found Madóran and Len already chowing down on chicken salad. There was a huge bowl of apricots on the table; one of Madóran's patients had paid with fruit and eggs. The apricots were rosy and perfect. I ate about ten of them along with my lunch.

"Lomen called," Len said. "They're in Albuquerque."

I looked up at her. "Lomen's got a phone?"

"I gave him mine," Caeran said.

"Have they seen Savhoran?"

Len shook her head. "They're going to stop by his place after sunset."

I took another bite of salad. I wanted to know about him *now*.

Madóran only had one more patient that afternoon, so Len and I worked on ælven some more, with Caeran's help. I loved just listening to him speak the language. I knew I wasn't pronouncing things right—there were nuances of inflection and stuff that were far more subtle than anything in English.

We worked until four, then sat in the *plazuela* until suppertime. Caeran chaperoned us, making me grateful yet again. Long ago—forever ago—I'd been jealous of him, but he had done me too many favors. I owed him.

We all gathered in the kitchen for supper, Mirali and Nathrin too. Mirali was moving a little slowly and she looked pale. She said something to Madóran in ælven and he answered. They spoke too fast for me, with my two lessons, to have a snowball's chance in hell of understanding. I looked at Caeran and saw a slight frown on his brow.

Mirali picked at her meal. I wondered if ælven pregnancies were like human pregnancies. They might have a whole different set of problems. It didn't surprise me when Madóran, Nathrin, and Mirali all left right after we finished eating.

Len, Caeran, and I cleaned up and put away the leftovers. While we were washing dishes Len's phone rang. She stepped aside to answer it and Caeran took her place at the sink.

I tried to listen, but Len's side of the conversation was mostly "Uh-huh" and "OK." When she hung up, she came back to the counter. Caeran looked at her and they had one of those long staring moments.

Len took the dish towel away from me. "Savhoran's not at home. They found his cell phone in his apartment."

Shit.

"They're going to look in the bosque, but they think he's been gone a while. There's no fresh khi in his place."

I frowned. "Fresh what?"

"Khi is the energy of a living being," Caeran said. "We leave traces of it wherever we go."

"Like chi," Len said. She turned to Caeran. "But there's also prime khi, right? That's different."

"Not really," he said. "The earth is a living being."

That didn't make a lot of sense to me, but I didn't really care. Savhoran was missing. That was what I cared about.

Len pushed a glass of ice water into my hand and nudged me toward the table. I sat down and stared out the window. Most of the *plazuela* was in shadow but a strip of flagstones at the east side were glowing golden in the setting sun.

Had he left New Mexico? He knew how his presence bothered the others. He might have decided to leave for their sake. But without even saying goodbye?

Len and Caeran were talking quietly and finishing up the dishes. I rubbed my eyes and drank some water, and tried to understand how Savhoran could just leave. He didn't know me that well; we'd only met a couple of months ago, and for an ælven that wasn't very long. And he didn't like the fact that he had to drink blood to survive.

My heart lurched as I thought that maybe he hadn't left at all, at least not that way. I closed my eyes, refusing to even think about that. Listened to Len and Caeran putting things away. Outside a bird gave a falling cry.

I heard someone sit across from me. I opened my eyes and saw Len looking at me, worried.

"We're done," she said. "Want us to walk you to your room?"

I nodded and stood, taking my water glass along. We went out to the *portal* and walked around to my room. I went in and said good night, then watched them walk around to the west side where their room was.

I sat on my bed and watched the garden slowly darken. Fought against the sadness.

Maybe Savhoran was just out hunting. Maybe he'd found a hot lead on the alben female. Maybe he'd found her hiding place and was staking it out.

The garden was getting hard to see. The bushes were just dark blobs now. I could just make out the patio furniture, and now and then I got a glint off the fountain's water. Was the moon up? I stood up to go look, and was halfway to my door when I saw someone jump into the *plazuela* and land silently, knees bent like it had just been a small jump.

A chill of fear shot through me. It was the alben female.

= 10 =

I could just make out her silhouette. She was looking around, peering through the glass walls. I dropped to a crouch behind my dresser. Stupid; she could probably tell I was there anyway, but it made me feel better.

She hadn't spotted me yet. I was debating whether she'd hear me if I did a mental shout out to Madóran when another person jumped down into the garden from the roof. Male, long hair, dark. He grabbed the female and they scuffled.

"Shit!"

I ran out into the *portal*, not caring anymore if I was seen. Looked around for something I could use as a weapon. Yeah, not bright, but I wanted to help.

The female tried to break away but he had her around the waist. Her struggles threw them off balance and they crashed into some of the patio furniture, making a racket. That ought to bring the others.

There was a bright flash of light, then a thump. I looked up.

The guy was on the ground. The female bent her knees and did a superman jump right out of the courtyard. I heard her land on the roof and run a few steps, then silence. She must have jumped down outside.

I ran to the nearest glass door and fumbled with the latch. Heard another door opening, voices. Didn't care. I got the latch open and went out.

The guy on the ground was struggling to get up. I hurried over to him, which was stupid if it was someone else, but I thought—hoped—

He looked up at me. I let out a gasp and dropped down beside him.

"Savhoran!"

I put my arms around him. He struggled against me, still trying to get up. I got it; I let go and he managed to stand, but when he tried to put his weight on both feet he cried out and started to fall. I caught him and helped him to a chair.

"She's gone," I said.

Caeran came running up to us. Savhoran still had his eyes squeezed shut and both hands wrapped around his shin. I looked up at Caeran, and he nodded.

"I'll get Madóran."

He spun and dashed back to the *portal*. I dragged another chair over, sat in it, put my arm around Savhoran's shoulders and laid my head against his back.

"I'm glad you're here. I was starting to wonder."

He didn't say anything. That was all right. I was just happy to be near him, relieved he was alive.

Gradually his breathing slowed. Len came out and put her hands over his, doing the healing thing I guess. Madóran must have taught her. I ignored a twinge of jealousy.

After a couple of minutes, Caeran came back with Madóran. I glanced up and saw Nathrin and Mirali on the *portal*, going back to their room.

Len stood up and Madóran took her place. He gently pulled Savhoran's hands away from his leg and put his own there. Savhoran leaned back and sighed. I felt a tingle in the air, and saw a faint glow around Madóran's hands.

"It is badly bruised, but not broken," he said. "Caeran, please get Savhoran a glass of water."

Caeran took off for the kitchen. Len pulled up another chair.

"What happened?" she asked.

I glanced at Savhoran, but his eyes were still closed.

"It was the alben, the female," I said. "She jumped into the *plazuela* from the roof and Savhoran came after her."

Len glanced at Savhoran. "How did they get here?"

"She followed Caeran and the others from the house in Albuquerque," Savhoran said, his voice tight. He was still frowning in pain, but he had opened his eyes. "She was tracking them, and I in turn tracked her."

"Why didn't you take your phone?" I asked.

"I could not go back for it. I would have lost her."

I smoothed his hair back from his face. He looked like hell, exhausted and in pain.

Caeran came with the water and Savhoran chugged it. Without a word, Caeran took the glass and went for more.

Savhoran took a couple of deep breaths. "I have failed. I am sorry."

I took his hand and he squeezed mine so hard I had to bite my lip to keep from complaining. It was good, though. It meant he wanted me to stay.

"It is not a failure," Madóran said. "Now we are aware of her presence."

"I had hoped to rid you of her presence."

"In time." Madóran held a hand over Savhoran's head. "How long is it since you last fed?"

Savhoran stared at the ground. My heart sank.

"Caeran and the guys left Albuquerque Friday night," Len said.

I nodded, remembering. The other alben—Pirian—had shown up that night and set everything off. It occurred to me that Savhoran didn't know about Pirian, but now was not the time to tell him.

Caeran came back, bringing the full glass and a pitcher of water. Savhoran drank two more glasses without stopping, then leaned back again and closed his eyes. He still gripped my hand.

"You cannot hunt in Guadalupita," said Madóran gently.

"I have no intention of hunting here," Savhoran answered.

"Where, then?"

"I do not know. Let me rest."

Madóran's brow creased with concern. He stood and summoned Caeran with a nod, and they both went into the *portal*. Len watched them go, frowning.

"Did you come all the way on foot?" I asked.

Savhoran nodded. I looked at his boots, which were just leather, like moccasins. I wondered if the soles were worn through.

"I'd better let Lomen know what's going on," Len said, getting up. She walked away and pulled her cell from her pocket.

Savhoran raised his head and looked at me. "Lomen is not here?"

"They decided to go back to Albuquerque to hunt the alben," I told him. "They must have passed you on the way."

"When did they leave?"

"Saturday. They took the bus from Las Vegas. They've been in Albuquerque a couple of days."

He frowned, and I wondered if he knew what a bus was. I felt sorry for him, having to deal with our world on top of being sick and having to hide the fact that he wasn't human.

He closed his eyes again. I put my hand on his forehead and was shocked at how cold it was. His hand was cold too; I just hadn't noticed. It scared me.

I am all right.

I caught my breath at the contact. He was definitely in pain, not only from the bruise but just a general ache and weariness, and hunger. *Serious* hunger. I understood the agony it caused him, physical and emotional. He must have been too tired to hide it from me.

I kissed his cheek and he let out a small sigh. He still gripped my hand; I put my other hand over his, trying to warm it.

I heard footsteps and looked up, expecting Len, but it was Madóran and Caeran. Madóran carefully carried a wooden cup in his hand. He walked right up and stood in front of Savhoran, and Caeran stopped beside him.

I knew, because we were still in contact, that Savhoran smelled the blood. His hunger flared, becoming unbearable. At the same time despair sank his heart. I felt tears running down my face.

He swallowed, eyes clenched shut, and whispered, "No."

"This is a gift," Madóran said. "It is from both of us."

Savhoran shook his head. "If I do this, I will truly be a monster."

"No," Madóran said. "You harm no one in accepting this."

"We cannot take it back," added Caeran.

Savhoran didn't answer. I felt his turmoil. I wanted to help but there was nothing I could do—it was his decision.

"You can still hunt the alben," Madóran said, "but only if you are strong."

Savhoran took a couple of breaths, then looked at me. His eyes sought my approval, my forgiveness.

I want you to live, I told him. *But I'll respect your choice.*

He gazed at me, still troubled but not as agitated. *You would not be disgusted with me?*

Of course not.

He lowered his gaze. *Others would.*

Well, that's their problem.

He closed his eyes and I felt a flicker of amusement. I squeezed his hand, then let go. He took a deep breath and accepted the cup from Madóran.

I was so tied into him that *I* wanted that cup of blood. I

felt his need for it, felt the physical urgency that drove him to compromise his ideals. He had no good choices.

He hesitated, then brought the cup to his lips. Instinct took over and he gulped greedily until he'd drained it, then gasped for breath.

The change was immediate. I felt it and was stunned by the difference that small amount of blood made. He was still hungry, but not unbearably so. The pain vanished, and strength flowed through him. His face took on color, as much as I could see in the light from the *portal*.

Savhoran held the cup out to Madóran and bowed his head. "I thank you."

"Keep the cup. It, too, is a gift. Such cups were used by Ebonwatch in their day."

Savhoran looked at the cup, tipped it up to catch the last drop it held, then cradled it in his lap. He sat thinking for a minute, and I realized I didn't know what about. Our contact had faded, or his renewed strength made it easier for him to shield his thoughts.

He looked up sharply. "I can still catch her."

He stood, but his injured leg buckled. I grabbed his arm to keep him from falling.

"I think a night and day of rest would be better for you," Madóran said. "Come. Your room is available."

We walked to his room, Savhoran leaning on me with his arm around my shoulders and the cup clutched in his free hand. He couldn't put much weight on the bad leg. Madóran had him sit on his bed and gave him another shot of healing, then went away, leaving the door open.

I'd been standing out of the way, watching. Now I sat next to Savhoran. I wanted to tell him I was proud of him, but I wasn't sure he'd like hearing that. He was staring at the cup, frowning.

"Are you angry?" I asked.

"Only with myself."

He put the cup on his nightstand. I leaned my head on his shoulder. He was tense; I didn't need telepathy to know that. After a minute he turned and took my face in his hands. He looked like he was about to say something, then with an exasperated little gasp he kissed me.

We'd kissed before, but not like this. He was hungry in a different way, and my body said yes. My thoughts flicked to the condoms I had stashed in my bag.

He drew back. "I should not do this."

"Why not?"

"I...have a task to complete." He slid his hand behind my neck, gazing at me through long lashes. "You are very tempting, but I must focus."

"You're not going anywhere tonight, right?"

He leaned his forehead against mine. "Madóran was right. I need rest. And you will need to sleep."

"It's early."

"Amanda—"

"OK, but can I just stay with you a while? I missed you. I'll just watch you rest."

He laughed softly, then gathered me into his arms. "I missed you too."

I closed my eyes and just concentrated on enjoying him. His arms around me—warm, now, not cold—his smell, the feel of his cheek against mine. We sat like that a long time.

Finally we let go. I looked up at him and saw that while he no longer looked like death warmed over, he did look tired and in need of some grooming. I touched his braid, which had wisps sticking out all along its length.

"May I brush it out for you?"

"I have no brush."

"I'll use mine. I'll go get it." I stood up.

"Let me come with you. You should not walk outside

alone."

That made me remember the alben. Would she come back tonight? I looked out at the *plazuela*, peaceful in the starlight.

Savhoran got to his feet and held out his hand. I put mine in it, but he was still limping a little so I pulled his arm around my shoulders again and we walked to my room.

He sat on my bed while I rummaged in my bag for my brush. Found it, sat behind him, and worked on undoing the narrow strip of soft leather that tied his hair. Took me a minute to get the knot undone. I set the leather aside and used my fingers to loosen the braid.

Savhoran's hair was soft and fine. As I worked it loose I saw a shock of white the width of my pinkie, and I gasped.

"What is it?"

I separated the white and draped it around in front of his shoulder. He touched it, then sighed.

I hugged his back. "I still love you. I'll always love you."

"Hush. We are not much more than strangers."

"We're a *lot* more."

I pushed his hair aside and kissed the back of his neck. He inhaled sharply. I kept going, savoring the salty, slightly musky taste of his skin. Yes, he could use a bath. I didn't care.

He turned and caught my hands, kissed each one. "Dearest Amanda. Not now."

I swallowed my disappointment. "OK. I'll just finish your hair."

I brushed it, gently working out the knots, enjoying its silkiness. The white all but disappeared when braided in with the rest of his hair. I wondered how long it would take the others to notice it.

I tied the braid off with the leather. Savhoran stood, a little unsteadily.

"Good night, Amanda."

I went with him to the door. "Can I visit you tomorrow? During the day, I mean. Or would it be bad to open your door?"

"Just give me warning."

I threw my arms around him and held tight. He returned the embrace, holding me tight enough to convince me he didn't consider me a stranger. Then he slipped away and limped down to his room. I watched until I heard the door close.

The *plazuela* was still except for the fountain. Remembering the alben, I closed my door and locked it.

I didn't sleep very well, between worrying about the alben and wishing I was with Savhoran. At least I knew where he was. When I woke up I wanted to run down to his room that minute, but I resisted. I got dressed, and by the time I was ready, Len and Caeran were at my door.

Nathrin and Mirali didn't show for breakfast. Madóran was fixing a tray for them when we came in. Over breakfast Len said that Lomen and the others were on their way back; Caeran would pick them up in Las Vegas that afternoon.

After eating too much, I worked with Madóran in the garden, though I would rather have been with Savhoran. Madóran had already seen him that day. He didn't volunteer any details, and I didn't ask. I decided not to bother Savhoran until after lunch. Madóran had plenty of stuff for us to do, watering and weeding, and tending the raspberry bushes he had growing toward the back of the house.

The raspberry patch was as big as the whole vegetable garden, almost as big as the vineyard. North of it and west of the house, the orchard stretched toward the foothills, sloping down toward a river and up again on the far side, only ending when it ran up against the forest. I saw what looked like a ruin back there under the pines, and asked Madóran what it was.

"A house, or rather the beginning of one. The work has been interrupted."

"Whose house? You've got a neighbor?"

He glanced at me under the brim of his hat. "The clan is building it. I invited them to do so."

I looked back at the house to be. "So it's on your land?"

"I have more than enough room."

"How far does your property go, anyway?"

He straightened and gazed toward the mountains. "Do you see that peak with the splash of aspens?"

"The lighter green? Yeah."

"It is part of my land."

"Damn! That's a lot of land!"

"I received a grant in 1660. Over the years, I have acquired adjacent lands when my neighbors chose to sell."

He'd been here over three hundred years. Yeah, I guess you could collect a lot of land in that amount of time.

We gave the raspberries a drink and went back in the house. "How do you harvest all the fruit from that orchard?" I asked as we put away hats and gloves.

"I get help from the village. Fruit for labor."

I followed him into the kitchen where we each chugged a couple of glasses of water. I offered to help fix lunch. Madóran declined, so I went to my room to clean up. I brushed my teeth, showered, even washed my hair. It still wasn't lunch time, so I gave in and went down the *portal* to Savhoran's room.

I stood in front of the door, debating whether I should leave him alone. I must have been thinking loud, because I heard him moving around.

Come in.

I opened the door and came face to face with a black, lacquered screen. Stepped in, pulled the door shut, and peeked around the screen.

Savhoran was lounging on his bed, reading a book. I'd never seen him do that before; it made me feel hopeful. I went over to him, about to ask what the book was, but I saw ælven lettering on the cover and decided not to.

It is the journal of a member of Clan Ebonwatch. Madóran thought I might gain some insight from it.

Makes sense.

I am not to read the final chapter, however. The author makes it her farewell; she decided to cross.

Yeah, don't read it.

I sat in the chair next to his bed. He put the book aside and turned to me. I realized he was wearing different clothes: dark green cotton tunic and pants. Madóran must have offered to wash his other stuff.

How's the leg?

Much better, thank you. Rest has made a great difference.

His hair was loose over his shoulders, and looked clean. Both of us freshly bathed. Hmm.

He smiled, and I realized I was still thinking too loud. "Sorry," I said.

I closed my eyes and tried to shield my thoughts. Too distracted. I could smell a familiar shampoo, the same I'd just used. I felt Savhoran's hand on my shoulder and looked at him.

He gave me a sweet kiss. I thought about the condoms sitting uselessly in my bag.

What is that?

Um, birth control.

Savhoran backed off. *I see.*

I can go get it. You're not offended, are you?

No.

It's not about the curse. I'd want birth control even if you didn't have it. I'm not ready for kids.

He gave a sad smile. *Your people conceive much more easily than mine. We would never wish to prevent it.*

The moment of passion was completely dead by now. I sighed.

I understand, Amanda.

If I wanted kids, I would want you to be the father, OK?

He looked away. *A different father would be a better choice.*

Oh, jeez. Could I screw this up any worse?

Someone who can be with you, help you raise the children.

OK, these children are just theoretical, right? You would be fine helping raise them.

I could not play with them outside, nor take them for outings during the day.

Neither of which is the end of the world.

I couldn't believe we were having this conversation. I moved to the bed, crowding against him, and put my arms around him.

I'm sorry I brought it up. Look, let's just forget it, OK?

He put his hand over mine. *It is good that we spoke of this. It means we both care.*

Of course I care.

He squeezed my hand. I closed my eyes, thinking how good it felt just to touch him. I was careful not to hide that thought.

A knock on the door made me jump. We both straightened up.

"Yes?" said Savhoran.

"Is Amanda with you?" said Caeran through the door.

"Yeah, I'm here," I said.

"Lunch is ready."

Crap. I turned to Savhoran. He looked amused.

Go on.

I'm coming back here after.

All right.

I kissed him, then went to the door. Len was waiting with

Caeran. We walked across to the kitchen, where we found Nathrin and Madóran having a heated discussion.

"She cannot stay in this house while he is here," Nathrin said as we walked in. He glanced at me and I knew exactly what he was talking about.

"And he cannot stay at the new house," Madóran said. "It is not secure. He would be vulnerable."

I sat at the table, helped myself to lemonade from the pitcher there, and spent ten seconds carefully walling my self around with white light. If, as I suspected, Nathrin had suggested that Savhoran leave the hacienda, he wouldn't have trouble guessing my opinion.

They dropped the subject, which was just as well. Nathrin went off with the tray Madóran had fixed, and the rest came and joined me at the table.

Lunch was gazpacho with bread and butter on the side. The cold soup was fantastic: salty, garlicky, and crunchy with cucumbers and tomatoes we'd picked that morning. I gobbled my bowl and said yes to seconds.

"Nathrin and Mirali could stay at our place in Albuquerque," Len said, buttering a piece of bread. "You wouldn't mind, right Caeran?"

"It is a good idea," he said. "I will offer it to them."

"That is generous of you both," Madóran said, "but will they be safe enough in Albuquerque? The alben knows where your house is, from what Savhoran told us."

"She is more interested in hunting us," said Caeran.

"How would they get there?" I asked. "By bus?"

Caeran nodded. "I could take them to Las Vegas this afternoon, when I go to pick up the others." He turned to Len, who already had her phone out, surfing the schedule.

"I think the bus left already," Len said. "Might have to be tomorrow."

I listened while they worked out the details, but my

thoughts had already wandered back to Savhoran. I could stop by my room after lunch for the condoms—but no. Today was not the day, not after that discussion of parenthood.

I swallowed, remembering Savhoran's dismay over what he felt was inadequacy. It wasn't his fault he couldn't go out in daylight. That wouldn't make him a bad father.

Not that I had any immediate desire for kids. My best friend in high school had gotten pregnant her junior year, and disappeared from school and from my life. I wanted some free years before I considered making a family.

I came back to the present when the others got up from the table. Madóran turned down my halfhearted offer to help with the dishes. I went out with Caeran and Len, but stopped at Savhoran's room, not mine. They didn't comment.

I spent the afternoon with Savhoran. We hugged and kissed a bit, but mostly we just talked. We skirted around dangerous topics. Instead we got better acquainted by sharing our pasts. I ran out of material first, of course. I had to nudge Savhoran to tell me more about himself.

He had been with the clan—which was much bigger than just the folks who were here in New Mexico—all his life. Most of it he'd spent in remote forests in eastern Europe. When remote stopped being so remote any more, he and the others came to America, following a rumor that Madóran had gone west with the Spanish colonists.

"Why were you interested in Madóran?" I asked. "Did any of you know him?"

"Caeran's mother knew him. She was his partner briefly, and remembered him fondly. The stories she told about him made Caeran want to meet Madóran."

"Is she still, um—"

"She crossed a few years ago."

"What about your parents?"

He shook his head. From the pain in his face, it was a bad

story. I didn't push for more.

We cuddled on his bed, and I actually fell asleep. I woke to voices outside on the *portal*. Lomen, Bironan, and Faranin were back.

We had supper in the great room again. Nathrin and Mirali stayed away, and the others talked about hunting the female alben. I was getting tired of listening to this kind of stuff.

"OK, look," I said when I couldn't stand it any longer. "You need to get methodical about this."

They stared at me like I was a Martian. Faranin frowned. Ignoring him, I took out my phone and surfed up a list of news stories about Campus Killer II.

"Let's look at the facts. She's killed four students now. All male. Those were food, but I'm different. She doesn't attack me because she's hungry."

"Vengeance," Len said.

"For what? What did I do to her?"

"Not you, Caeran. He kept her from getting to you."

I narrowed my eyes. "So I was *supposed* to be food, and he prevented it, and she's mad? She followed me all the way up here because of that?"

Caeran didn't say anything. I was pretty sure there was more to it, but he wasn't going to help.

"All right," I said. "Let's look at when and where she hunts. Maybe there's a pattern."

"In Albuquerque," Len said, "but she's here now."

"She could go back. Maybe we should lead her back."

I scrolled through the news stories and made a list of the dates and locations where bodies had been found. Might not do any good, but at least I was doing something.

"Three of the four victims were found on campus or near it," I announced.

The fourth was a short distance away—Roosevelt Park—

but that was kind of scary close to Caeran's house. Avoiding that, I added the attacks on me to the list.

"Then she tried to jump me at the movie theater parking lot, the casino, and in the library bathroom."

"The first was spur-of-the-moment," Len said. "She caught a whiff of you and ran to catch you."

"So could the second," Lomen said. "She could have followed us to the casino, watched us sign up for the poker game and known we would be there later in the evening. All she had to do was hide in the restroom."

I nodded. "The library was trickier, but not much. She would have had to stalk me in the daytime to know I was working there." I paused; that thought kind of freaked me out. Took a sip from my water glass.

"Once she knew that, again, all she had to do was hide out in the restroom," said Caeran.

I was never going in a public restroom again unless I had a friend along and a can of pepper spray in my hand.

I looked over the whole list. "She only hunts me when she isn't hungry."

Caeran nodded. "It makes sense. Hunger distracts her, weakens her. She plans her hunting for sustenance at times and locations where she is safe."

"Where is she least safe?" I asked.

"In a large crowd of people. Outdoors in daylight."

I thought wistfully of an endless baseball game. It would be the perfect hideout.

"So...the best time to hunt her would be when she is hungry. Because then she will probably be somewhere near campus or University Heights." I glanced at the dates in my list. "Looks like that's about every two weeks."

"But she is here now, not on campus," said Lomen.

"Yeah, and she's not hungry. Well, since we don't know how she behaves under those circumstances, I suggest we go back to where we do know how she behaves. Back to Albuquerque."

The ælven exchanged long looks. Caeran shrugged.

"It would get her away from Mirali."

They proceeded to go over my entire argument again, pulling it apart, trying to find flaws. I told them, on demand, the dates of the killings. I was getting annoyed at their method of problem-solving, so when the meal was over I headed back to Savhoran's room. I had only been there for a short while—long enough for the sun to set—when Madóran and Len knocked on the door, wanting to give Savhoran another treatment.

I could go back to my room, or hang out in the great room and listen to the men arguing. Despite the annoyance factor, I opted for the great room. Didn't really feel like being alone.

Savhoran walked me to the door and gave me a long kiss that set my thighs tingling.

Come get me when you're done, I told him.

He smiled, kissed me again, and left. I watched him walk around to the treatment room and go in.

Caeran was still sitting at the table with the other three. He glanced up as I passed on my way to the couch. With no Len to talk to, I got bored pretty fast and wandered out into the entryway where I could look through the window out at the *plazuela*.

The alben had jumped down into it last night. Pretty bold, but then Savhoran had surprised her and she took off. She would never have come into the *plazuela* if she'd known he was around. He'd almost had her.

Twilight was fading into evening. I just saw vague shapes of bushes, and the fountain. She could be hiding out there for all I knew.

A pounding on the front door made me jump. I turned,

wondering if I should go find Madóran—except he didn't like being bothered when he was working. I took a few steps toward the door and the pounding came again.

Caeran came out of the great room. "Stay back," he said, going to the door.

There was a little hatch in the door, like in old comedy movies of speakeasies. Caeran opened it and looked out. I heard a man's voice speaking Spanish; something about chickens. Caeran answered him, then opened the door and went out.

I tiptoed to the door to see what was going on. The visitor, a stocky Hispanic, had a wheelbarrow full of what looked like a couple dozen dead chickens. The smell made me gag. While Caeran was arguing with him about what to do with the dead birds, I wandered out onto the *portal*.

I moved away along the front of the house, looking at the early stars. All the defensive stuff we'd been doing since we'd come there drained out of my brain. All I was thinking was how pretty the sky was.

I stepped off the porch. That made me remember that I shouldn't be outside.

The freeze got me before I could think about wanting help.

= 11 =

I kept walking, though I no longer wanted to, out into the field in front of Madóran's house. Caeran was still arguing with the chicken guy. His voice faded behind me. Tears slid down my face.

I got all the way to the fence by the road before I saw her. Just a silhouette, but I already knew it was her. She had taken no chances of being seen, the opposite of last night's approach.

I struggled to resist, but the only result was that my walking became clumsier, zombie-like. She made me walk right up to the fence. She was standing outside it. She stared at me for what seemed like an hour.

The moon wasn't up so I couldn't see her face very well. I could feel what she thought about me, though, and it wasn't pleasant.

Climb over.

I shivered at the touch of her thought. I didn't want to obey; I struggled again to break free.

The freeze came back, only it was pain. I couldn't move, couldn't even close my eyes. Had to keep looking at her smug face.

Unless you want more, you will climb.

I climbed. I thought she was going to kill me right then but she marched me up the road in front of her, northward.

Not seeing her was worse. The back of my neck felt like a thousand ants were crawling on it.

I don't know how long we walked, but by the time we turned off the road toward the mountains my feet were hurting. There was no fence this far from the village. Walking over the open ground was rougher and a couple of times I almost fell. No sympathy from the bitch.

I thought about Savhoran, how I wished I could say goodbye to him. Wished I'd picked up the damn condoms. Life was too short, and now mine was *really* too short.

I thought about his kisses. I didn't care if the bitch heard. I hoped she did—hoped she knew how much more Savhoran would hate her for this. He would kill her, I knew it. I was just sorry I wouldn't see it.

We reached the foothills and started climbing. My legs ached and she prodded me with a pain zap now and then. I wondered why she was bothering to go so far.

By that time I was so tired I stopped thinking about much besides putting one foot in front of the other. I kept my eyes on the ground to keep from tripping.

All I remember is a lot of pine trees, and climbing around rocks up the side of a canyon, and then a cave. We had to duck to go in. An uncomfortable place to die, but I was so tired I didn't care anymore. I just wanted to sit down.

She let me do that while she stood at the cave's entrance, watching for pursuit I guess. I leaned against the cave wall and closed my eyes.

Not much longer now. So long, Mom and Dad. So long, bro. Hope you all do better than me.

I woke with an aching butt and a crick in my neck. The little bit of sky I could see through the entrance was gray. I thought at first it was twilight, then remembered it had almost been dark when the alben caught me.

Fear flooded through me. I glanced sidelong back into the cave. She was there; I didn't see her but I knew.

I was maybe five strides from the entrance. Too far. I'd never make it.

I sat watching the sky grow lighter, wondering why I

wasn't dead. Maybe she wasn't hungry, was all I could think of.

She chuckled.

I squeezed my eyes shut and concentrated on white light. Tried to blank everything else out of my thoughts.

That is useless.

I flinched, hating the feel of her in my mind. I went limp, playing dead, hoping maybe if I was boring she'd ignore me. I couldn't help the tears, but maybe if I held still she wouldn't notice.

Something scraped back in the cave. Might have been just her foot, but the sound made me open my eyes. My gaze was drawn outside again, to the world I couldn't get back to. It was getting brighter. The sun would rise soon.

A scrub jay flew past the cave's entrance, then scolded from somewhere uphill. A minute later I heard a sliding sound, as if someone had taken a bad step. I didn't hear any more footsteps, but a few seconds later the view was blocked by a man.

He was backlit so I couldn't see who it was. I felt anger from the alben behind me.

The man spoke in ælven. I recognized his voice but couldn't place it. Not Caeran, not Lomen...

He came in slowly, walking past me as if I didn't exist. I caught a glimpse of white hair.

Great.

I looked after him into the cave, but couldn't see because daylight had contracted my pupils. I kept my gaze away from the entrance, hoping my eyes would adjust.

I heard him sit down. The female said something in a snide tone. The guy answered more moderately. I got the impression he was trying to persuade her of something. She continued to be snotty.

After a while he got less patient. My heart beat faster as

the volume increased. The air started prickling.

My eyes had adjusted enough that I could see them a little. Both were on their feet now. I was trying to see her face when a flash of light blinded me.

Shouting. Scuffling. I crawled toward the cave entrance, too blind to stand yet. There was another flash behind me and then I was out, free!

My legs were stiff and sore from the long hike in. I forced myself to scramble down the cliff to the bottom of the canyon. There was a stream bed with barely a trickle in it. I stumbled along that for a while. When I couldn't go any farther I hid behind a boulder and took out my phone.

No bars. Too much mountain around me. I rested a little, listening for pursuit, but it was quiet. They'd risk sun damage if they came out.

When I'd caught my breath, I continued following the stream. I didn't have a clear idea where I was, but it was probably north and west of Guadalupita. Eventually the stream should take me to the Mora River.

The ground got less steep and less rocky. The canyon widened out to a gentler valley, and the stream meandered back and forth across its bottom. I must have stepped over the water a dozen times.

I stopped to rest and try the phone again. This time I got a signal. I dialed Len, but Caeran answered.

"Manda! Where are you?"

"Um, not sure. In the foothills. I'm walking east, mostly. Following a creek."

"We will come find you. Keep talking."

Over the phone I heard an engine starting. He must have been in Len's car. I chattered inanely about the ground in front of me, as if by describing it I could tell Caeran where I was. He said encouraging things now and then. I was grateful for that.

The adrenaline had worn off. I realized I was hungry and thirsty. I kept walking, phone in hand. I was out in the open and that worried me, but the sun beating down on me was reassuring.

I came to an apple orchard and stopped under a tree, grateful for the shade. The apples were still green or I'd have been all over them. I sat with my back against a tree trunk and called Caeran.

"I'm in an apple orchard."

"Thank you. That is helpful."

"Is Len with you?"

"She is back at the house."

I closed my eyes. So tired.

"We have just come to an orchard. Wave your arms."

"OK, but I'm at the back."

I got to my feet and waved, phone on my shoulder.

"I see you. Wait there."

I sat down again, relieved. Adventure over.

Now all I needed to do was make sure the alben never found me again. Move to Montana, maybe.

In a couple of minutes, Caeran came running up. I stood up. He knelt on one knee and bowed his head.

"Forgive me. My inattention caused this."

"Not your fault."

He looked up at me with troubled eyes. I was too tired for an angsty discussion.

"Really, it's OK. Let's just go."

He nodded, and before I could blink he scooped me up in his arms and started across the orchard. I was too tired and grateful to protest.

I saw Len's car on the road outside the orchard's fence. Lomen and Bironan were standing next to it. Caeran set me down by the driver door and handed me the keys.

"Can you drive?"

"Uh..."

"Wait here, then. If you feel up to it later, drive back to the hacienda. Savhoran is anxious to see you."

Savhoran. I was suddenly glad it was daylight, or he'd be here looking for blood. So to speak.

"The alben is still in the mountains?" Caeran asked.

I nodded. "In a cave. The other alben is there too."

Caeran's eyes widened. "Pirian?"

"Yeah. They got into an argument. That's how I got away."

"Will you allow me to see what you saw of this place?"

"Um, sure I guess. What do I have to do?"

Caeran laid his hand on my shoulder. "Just remember."

I could feel the tingle from his hand sinking into me. Felt good. I had to concentrate to bring up the memories. I didn't remember the journey in to the cave very well, but I remembered getting out. I thought about it, and about the two alben in the cave, until Caeran let me go.

"Lock yourself in," he said.

I did. I cracked the windows and watched the four of them run across the orchard. When I lost sight of them, I looked around.

Caeran had parked the car on a strip of grass alongside the road. I could see a house up ahead, and that was reassuring. If I felt scared I could drive there, maybe. I was still pretty shaky.

I closed my eyes and tried to relax. It was broad daylight, and there were now four ælven between me and the alben. I told myself I was safe. Didn't believe it.

I dozed a little, but it wasn't good sleep. I kept remembering the cave, and the awful hike that had taken me there. The alben's creepy laugh.

My phone rang. I jumped so hard I would have hit the roof if I hadn't buckled myself in out of habit. With shaking hands, I got it out. Len's number.

"We need Madóran," Caeran said. "Can you get the car back to the hacienda? Len can bring him here."

I took a deep breath. "OK."

"Thank you. I will call and let them know you are coming."

I put the phone back in my pocket. Had to hunt for the keys; I'd had them in my hand, but must have dropped them when I was dozing. I found them in the footwell and managed to get the car key into the ignition.

The feel of the engine rumbling was actually reassuring. I still felt timid, but I managed to get the car pointed in the right direction with a K turn, and cruised back toward the hacienda.

I almost missed the turn. If it wasn't for the big carved owl on the gatepost I would have. I turned up the driveway and rolled along to the house. They must have been waiting, because they came out before I'd shut off the engine.

Len came to the driver door and tried to open it. I unlocked it and got out. She grabbed me in a hug as soon as I stood.

"Are you OK?"

"Yeah. Just sore from walking, and kind of freaked out."

She kissed my cheek. "Gotta go. We'll talk later."

Madóran was already in the passenger seat. Len hopped in and pulled away, leaving me standing outside.

Didn't want to be outside.

I hurried into the house. Savhoran was waiting in the great room, and hugged me so hard I couldn't breathe. For the first time since last night, I felt safe.

We sat on the couch and I told him what had happened. He looked so angry it scared me.

"Why did they need Madóran?" I asked, hoping to distract him. "Was someone hurt?"

"Pirian. They found him in the cave you described. The female was not there."

"That means she went out in the sun!"

"She can bear it better than I," he said grimly.

I hugged him. He held me and kissed me and I started to relax.

"Why did you go outside last night?" he asked.

"I think she made me. I didn't realize it until it was too late. I'm not that stupid."

Savhoran squeezed my hand. "She had control of the man with the chickens as well."

"So he was the distraction."

Savhoran nodded. "A clever one."

I leaned my head on his shoulder. So tired.

He stroked my hair. It felt good. I must have been a mess, but he didn't seem to care.

My stomach growled. I sat up. "Hungry."

We went to the kitchen. I went in first and drew the curtains over the windows.

Savhoran made me sit at the table and brought me food and drink—bread, cheese, water, milk, berries—until I told him to stop. When I wasn't gobbling we talked about the alben. The hunting was still coming up blank, and he was annoyed that she'd gotten so close to the house without their noticing.

"We need a different strategy," he said.

I nodded and swallowed a mouthful of bread. "Guns."

He gave me a skeptical look. "Do you know how to use one?"

"Point and shoot. How hard can it be?"

"Do you know how we can get them?"

"Well, they cost a lot. And you have to get a license. Maybe a background check. OK, bad idea."

He took my hands in his. "We will search tonight near

that cave. She will still be recovering from sun poisoning."

"Um. I'm not going to tell you not to kill her, but be careful, OK?"

He kissed me. "I will be careful, if only so that I can see you again."

"You can see me all you want."

We went back to the great room and cuddled on the couch. I fell asleep in his arms. Didn't wake up until I heard the front door open.

I sat up, heart pounding. Savhoran's hands soothed me. Madóran came in, followed by Caeran carrying someone wrapped up in a dark cloak. They hurried through to the far door that led to the *portal* by the treatment room. Len came in after them.

"Is that him?" I asked her.

"Yes. He's in bad shape. Madóran wants me to help."

"Where are the rest of the guys?"

"Looking for the female. If they can find where she's hiding now, while she's vulnerable..."

I glanced at Savhoran. He was frowning. He wanted to kill her himself.

Selfishly, I hoped they found her before nightfall.

Len headed for the treatment room. I settled back into Savhoran's arms and dozed some more.

This time it was evening when I woke. I was lying on my bed, alone. I rolled over and looked at the clock: eight thirty. I sat up.

Really stupid, but I was scared to leave the room. I thought about calling someone on the phone, but jeez, how embarrassing!

Suck it up, Richards. Be an adult.

A shower would make me feel better. I got up and took some fresh clothes from my dresser, opened my door a crack and stared out at the *plazuela* for a long time until I was convinced no alben was hiding out there, then scurried to the bathroom. Yes, I locked the door.

Hot water does wonderful things for the soul. I scrubbed all over and washed my hair, then stood with the water running on the backs of my aching thighs. Got out, toweled off, and dressed. I'd forgotten a comb, so I ran my fingers through my hair.

Again, I opened the door cautiously. All was calm in the *plazuela*. I put my dirty clothes in my room, then made a dash for the door into the great room.

Deserted. What time was it? I'd left my phone in my room. I could hear Len telling me how stupid that was, and by the way where was my pepper spray?

Madóran didn't have any clocks in the room. In fact, I didn't remember seeing any clocks in the house.

I went through the entryway and along into the kitchen. No one there either, but there was a note on the counter and a plate covered with a cloth napkin. The note, from Madóran, said here was some cake for me, and there was roast chicken in the fridge if I needed a meal.

I ate the cake first. Life's too short.

Good cake, too. Kind of a fruitcakey loaf, but much better than human-style fruitcake.

I didn't need more food, but I wanted a drink, so I looked in the fridge and found some milk. Poured myself a big glass and sat at the table.

The curtains were still over the windows. I pushed them aside and looked out at the garden. Feeling trapped again, and kind of lonely.

There was a short little hallway west of the kitchen. It led to the utility room and storage rooms, with door at the far end. I'd never been through that door.

I finished my milk and washed my dishes, then went down the hall to the door and knocked. Madóran answered, and smiled.

"Feeling better?"

"Much. Thanks for the cake."

The room behind him was gorgeous. Carved furniture—bed, nightstand, dresser, wardrobe—more ornate than anything else in the house. Blue bedspread with green and gold leaves all over it. Beautiful woven hangings on the walls. A chandelier of oil lamps filling the place with the scent of sandalwood.

"Would you like to come in?"

I woke up. "Sorry. It's just so glorious."

"Thank you."

He gestured a welcome, so I stepped in and looked around. There were ornaments everywhere: blown glass globes, ceramic figures, candle holders. I could have spent hours just looking at everything.

I turned to Madóran. "Where is everyone?"

His smile faded. "Out hunting, except for Len."

I swallowed. "So they didn't find her."

"No."

"What about the alben guy?"

"He is resting."

"Can I see him? I just want to thank him. I'm pretty sure he saved my bacon."

"Perhaps tomorrow. He is still rather weak."

"What did she do to him, anyway?"

Madóran's expression went grim. "She fed on his khi. It is against our creed to do so, but the alben do not follow the creed."

"Except Savhoran."

"I do not consider Savhoran alben."

That made me feel good. "Does he know that?" I asked.

"I suppose I have not said so. I assumed he knew."

"Tell him. Please."

He nodded. "You are right, I should. And now you would like to see Len, I imagine."

He walked across the room to another door. I followed him through it into a smaller room with a couch and a couple of chairs, lit by candles. Madóran went to another door in the right hand wall and knocked.

"Len? Amanda is here."

Len opened the door and grabbed me in a huge hug. We sat together on her and Caeran's bed and talked through everything. She had actually helped Madóran treat the alben.

"He was in really tough shape," she said. "I wasn't sure he'd make it. Madóran gave him a lot of energy and he's still weak."

"I'm feeling confused about him. I mean, he did try to whammy us right at first, but he also saved my butt this morning."

Len smiled. "He's all right, I think. Madóran isn't nervous about him. Of course, Madóran wants to think the best of everyone."

We kept talking until I noticed Len was yawning a lot. I stood up.

"Guess I should go—let you get some sleep."

"Stay if you want."

I hesitated. "Won't Caeran mind?"

"He'll be out all night. You missed a big rally meeting. They did everything but beat drums and put on war paint."

She got up and fetched two jumbo t-shirts from the dresser. "Night shirt," she said, handing me one.

We climbed into bed together and kept talking. Gradually Len drifted to sleep, and I lay there listening to her breathing, grateful not to be alone.

I slept too, even though I'd had a long nap. Stress will do that to you.

I dreamed about the alben guy. He brought me a big

bouquet of roses. Savhoran was jealous. I held the roses close to smell them and pricked my finger on a thorn. The alben guy grinned.

I woke with a start. Dark in the room, but there was a little light leaking in around the window curtains. Len was still asleep, so I held still and listened to birds chirping out in the garden. Finally I got up and pulled on my clothes.

Len rolled over. "Hm?"

"Gotta pee. Go back to sleep."

I wasn't quite brave enough to go all the way around to my room on the *plazuela*, so I went through the sitting room and knocked on Madoran's door. No answer. I opened the door a crack.

The room was empty. Pale light filtered through gauze at the windows; heavier drapes were pulled aside. I resisted the urge to explore and went through to the far door. In the hallway by the utility room was another bathroom. I used it, then went to the kitchen to peek out the window.

The sun wasn't up yet. Everything was shaded blue with the pre-dawn light. The garden was just as beautiful as always in this half-shadowed state. As I stood admiring it, I heard the front door open and close.

The hunters were home. I was just wearing panties and Len's shirt. I beat it back to her bedroom and scrambled into my clothes.

Len sat up and rubbed her eyes. "What's up?"

"They're back."

She slid out of bed and got dressed, and together we went back to the kitchen. Madóran was there, cooking up a huge breakfast of huevos, chorizo, and fresh-made tortillas. He instantly recruited us to help. Len filled the tea kettle while I cut up cantaloupe. Before I was done the clan straggled in.

They looked tired and disappointed. No one asked; there

was no need.

Len poured tea for them. I carried the plate of melon to the table and they all reached for it, even Savhoran. I watched, fascinated, while he ate the first solid food I'd seen him consume since he'd come down with the curse.

They were going through the melon fast, so I went and cut up another one. By that time Madóran had the eggs and sausage ready, and the guys lined up at the counter, except for Savhoran. He headed for the great room. I followed and caught up with him in the entryway.

"Hey," I said. "I missed you."

He glanced at the windows and beckoned me into the great room, where he caught me in a fierce hug. I hugged him back, breathing in the smell of him.

"You'll get her."

He sighed. "We found where she spent the day up a tree. She must have been badly sun-poisoned. We tracked her deep into the mountains, then her trail just disappeared."

"Maybe she quit and went home."

"She will not quit."

I leaned back and stroked his cheek. He looked strained.

"You need to hunt for yourself," I said, then bit my lip, afraid he'd be angry. He just looked depressed.

I kissed him all over his face, and finally he kissed me back. My loins started to tingle.

He pulled back. "The sun will rise soon. I need to get to my room."

"Can I come with you?"

"You may walk with me there."

I settled for that. He really did look exhausted. At the door to the *portal*, he peered warily out before going through it. He hurried to his room, two doors down, and went inside fast. I almost didn't make it through the door before he slammed it.

The room was dark. I blinked, waiting for my eyes to adjust.

"You should go," he said. "You are hungry."

"It's OK."

"No, it is not. Your hunger sharpens mine."

"Oh! I'm sorry!" I reached for the door. "Can I come back later?"

"Not today, love."

Love. I shivered. I reached out for him, groping because I couldn't see. He folded me in his arms, sweet and gentle. I wanted to stay there forever.

Amanda.

Boom, he was there, sexy and tired and incredibly hungry. So bad it hurt.

All, right, I'll go. I just don't want to. You know, we need to make a date to spend some time together without worrying about anything.

Until we catch the alben—

Yeah, I know.

I kissed him, then turned and felt my way to the door. "See you."

I walked around the *portal* to the kitchen, caution be damned. I was full of conflicting feelings. Sick of hiding, sick of waiting for the clan to catch the alben, and really sick of not having any quality time with Savhoran. I looked through the glass across the *plazuela* at his door, then went back to the kitchen.

Len was making more tortillas. The guys were lining up for seconds, and Madóran was cracking more eggs. I got in line behind them and got the last of round two. Looked at Len, who smiled and handed me a hot tortilla.

"I've had some," she said. "Want tea?"

I nodded, mouth already full. She poured mugs for both of us and refilled Madoran's, then she and I brought spare chairs over to the table and squished in. We all sat with elbows bumping and chairs crammed together. Nobody minded.

There was no discussion of what to do next. Granted, the guys were busy eating, but there was a sense of hopelessness in the air.

Madóran brought the cast-iron skillet full of eggs over and put it in the center of the table. He helped himself to a portion, took a tortilla from the basket, and leaned against the wall by the window to eat.

"We should go back to Albuquerque," I said. "We know her pattern there."

"It might be better to adopt a defensive strategy," Madóran said, poking at his eggs with his fork. "You all could use some rest. Perhaps remaining here for a few days would benefit you."

"Perhaps," Bironan said, "But we will post watchers. Shifts of two."

"One in the courtyard, one in front?" Lomen asked.

Bironan nodded. I had a feeling he wasn't including Savhoran in the plan. The thought made me mad but I kept it to myself. It wasn't a time for quarrels.

"What if she starts killing your neighbors?" I said to Madóran.

He gave me a pained look, but said nothing. I took a pull at my tea, gathering courage to make a suggestion. I'd been thinking of it ever since my impromptu hike, and while it made my belly go cold, I thought I had to offer.

"Maybe we should set a trap with me as the bait," I said. "I could go outside—"

"Oh, no," Len said. "We tried that last fall. Not a good idea."

"This is not Gehmanin," Madóran said quietly.

"Still not a good idea. She's evil," Len said.

"I've seen grad students who were worse," I said.

I meant it as a joke, but it fell horribly flat. They all stared, and I felt my face going red.

"What we must do is determine what she wants," Madóran said. "then we can either give it to her, or offer her a compromise."

Caeran frowned. "She wants Amanda."

Faranin shook his head. "Vengeance."

"For what?" I asked.

Long pause. Madóran put his plate on the corner of the table. He looked a little ill.

"For Gehmanin's death," he said.

Everyone was silent.

I knew less about the whole Gehmanin thing than the rest of them. The one thing I did know was that it was the biggest event that had happened since the clan first came to New Mexico.

"It would help, then, to know who she is," Caeran said.

Madóran sighed. "There are those we can contact to ask. I have not kept in touch with them, but some of you may know them."

Faranin shifted. "I know a few with kindred among the alben."

"Yes."

"They do not use...human technology. One of us would have to travel to contact them."

"No," Caeran said. "We need everyone here."

The discussion started going in circles. I got up and began clearing empty plates. Len came and joined me and we cleaned up the kitchen while the others argued. Finally the clan left to go look for clues in Madóran's library, leaving Madóran sitting alone at the table.

He looked dejected. Len brought him a fresh mug of tea. He still hadn't finished his breakfast.

We sat with him and waited. Finally he sighed.

"I have not wanted to rekindle old ties. I severed them purposely when I came here."

"You don't have to," Len said.

"Not even to resolve this?"

"They'll catch her or she'll get bored and go away. One or the other, eventually."

"I would like to believe that."

I didn't have anything to add. I looked out at the garden, wishing it didn't feel like no man's land. Middle of the day, and I was scared to go out there.

"Um, Madóran? Could we maybe go see the, ah—the guy?"

"Pirian? Yes, I should check on him. If you are willing to leave should I ask it, you may come with me."

"Sure."

We walked Len to her room first, then went around the *portal* to the treatment room. Madóran put his hands on the door and stood there for a minute, then nodded and opened it.

A chill of confusion went through me: fear at the sight of the alben warring with the amazing sexiness of him. Even lying sick in bed, even with the white hair that screamed "danger," he radiated attraction. It must have been a natural gift.

His eyes were closed. Madóran went the the foot of the bed and stood there. After a moment, the alben looked up at him, then at me. I glanced away.

"Pirian, this is Amanda," Madóran said. "She has something to say to you."

I dared to look at the alben again. One of his eyebrows was higher, and the feeling his gaze gave me wasn't nice this time. I wanted to run like a frightened deer. He was hungry.

I looked at my feet and cleared my throat. "I don't know

why you came to the cave," I said, "but you pretty much saved me, I think. So I wanted to thank you."

"I had no intention of saving you," he said. His voice was rough.

"I know," I told him. "I'm still grateful."

He laughed, which made me look up again. "The hen is grateful to the fox."

I didn't like being mocked. All at once I was no longer bothered by his pheromones.

I glared at him. "Who is she?"

He gave me a measuring look. "Her name is Kanna, though that means little to you."

I heard Madóran draw a sharp breath. Ignored it and kept my gaze on Pirian.

"What does she want?"

"I should think that was obvious."

"But why? She's gone to way more trouble than she'd need to get a meal."

"True." He went into a coughing fit. Madóran propped him up with pillows and gave him a glass of water from the nightstand.

I crossed my arms and stood waiting. I was mad. Underneath I was still scared, but damned if I was going to let it show.

Madóran said something to him in ælven. Pirian's answer was no; I caught that much. He drank some more water, then lay back on the pillows and looked at me through his eyelashes.

"She is kin to Gehmanin."

I glanced at Madóran. His turn to stare at the floor.

"So she's here for him?" I asked.

"She lost contact with him. She is convinced that Caeran is responsible."

"What?" I said. "Why Caeran?"

"Apparently Gehmanin told her that Caeran was his enemy."

Madóran said something in ælven again. I really needed to study some more. I hated being left out.

Pirian frowned and didn't answer. I got the feeling he didn't like what Madóran had said.

"So why did you go to the cave?" I asked.

Pirian's gaze shifted to me. "To share with Kanna the news that Gehmanin is dead. She was...unhappy."

I remembered how unhappy. The phrase "don't kill the messenger" came to mind.

"So now she wants to kill everybody here?"

"I believe she is now focused on Madóran."

I narrowed my eyes. My gut told me that Pirian had told her something to make her fix on Madóran. If Madóran was hurt because of him...

"What about you?" I asked him. "Are you on her side?"

"I am on no one's *side*. I meant to end it by telling Kanna what happened to Gehmanin. I thought she would be inclined to give up her vengeance, but it seems I misjudged her."

He started coughing again. Madóran gave me a look and I left, closing the door softly behind me.

I was out on the *portal* alone. Middle of the day, but it still gave me the creeps. I ducked into the my room and got my pepper spray and returned to the treatment room, standing there staring at the door, listening for any sound of trouble. After a minute I heard Madoran's voice, speaking ælven.

I went back to my room, closed the door, sat on the bed. And realized I'd rather be with Savhoran.

I argued with myself for a while. I should leave him alone—let him rest—but I didn't want to.

I shoved the pepper spray in my pocket and went out again.

Savhoran's room was two doors down from mine. I took a slow breath and looked out at the garden. It was peaceful. No one there, no one on the roof that I could see.

I walked to Savhoran's room and leaned my head against the door, as if I could do whatever Madóran had done earlier, which I didn't even know what it was. After a minute I felt so stupid I decided to just knock and apologize if I disturbed Savhoran. I was raising my hand when he called to me to come in.

I went in and he closed the door. No light in the room. I felt my way around the screen and stepped past it, but my eyes hadn't adjusted and I was afraid of tripping over something. I stood still.

I heard a small sound like cloth moving, then his arms were around me. I buried my face in his chest and took a deep breath.

"Hope I didn't bother you," I said.

For answer he kissed me. My hormones flared and I plastered myself against him. After a minute he gently guided me to the bed. To my disappointment, we just sat on it. He snaked his fingers through mine.

I felt hungry. It confused me, because breakfast hadn't been that long ago, then I realized it was probably Savhoran's hunger leaking over to me.

I found his face and kissed it. "You need food."

"I will hunt tonight. Perhaps the others will wait for me."

"They're not going out tonight. Change in strategy; they're going defensive, at least for a few days."

He sighed. "She may get away."

"So? If she leaves, good riddance."

His thumb stroked the back of my hand. I snuggled closer.

"But we will always worry that she will return," he said. "We must stop her now. It is the only way."

"She's here after Madóran," I told him. I was hoping to distract him from his own vendetta.

"How do you know that?"

"Pirian told me."

Savhoran grabbed my shoulders—a bit roughly, though he didn't quite shake me. "You talked to Pirian?"

"Madóran was there," I said hastily. "I just wanted to thank the guy for giving me the chance to escape."

"I wish you had waited for me."

"I kind of wanted to get it over with. He gives me the creeps."

Savhoran let go, only to put his arm around me. "He is dangerous. He does not wish you well."

"Yeah, I got that impression."

He squeezed my shoulders, then after a minute he said, "Why is she after Madóran?"

"She—her name is Kanna, by the way—she's related to Gehmanin. He told her he was coming to see Madóran, and Pirian told her Gehmanin's dead. She must have put two and two together and come up with five."

Savhoran didn't say anything for a long time. Thinking, I figured. I leaned my head on his shoulder. He kissed me, so sweetly I felt like crying, then drew back.

You should go.

I didn't want to. I took a breath, hugged him tight, then got up and stumbled my way to the door. I bumped into the screen and almost knocked it over.

Amanda...

What?

I love you.

I wanted to run back to him and jump his bones. That would just bother him, so I stayed where I was.

I love you too.

I felt a flood of warmth—physical and emotional—so

strong it took my breath away. Took an effort to make myself find the door handle.

I'm going, but not because I want to.

I know.

Once you've—hunted, lets spend some time together, OK?

He didn't answer right away. He hated the whole idea of hunting, I was sure. It was really just a polite term for something pretty awful.

I would like that.

I knew that was all I was going to get. I opened the door and slipped out.

A rush of fear went through me as I realized I hadn't checked first. Fortunately, the garden and the *portal* were uninhabited. I hurried to my room, sprawled on my bed, and fantasized about Savhoran until someone knocked on my door.

"Man?" Len called through the door. "Lunch time."

Lunch was subdued. The clan came and got plates and took them away to the library. I was a little offended, but Madóran and Len didn't seem to care.

After we cleaned up, Madóran fetched a couple of books and the three of us worked on ælven in his little sitting room. The afternoon went by fast. I felt like I was starting to get the hang of it.

Len and I helped fix supper. Madóran had us set the table in the great room. Over dinner, they discussed the watch schedule. Madóran was going to share watches in the *plazuela* with Caeran while the other three watched outside. Caeran offered to take the second shift.

"Savhoran can help," I said.

Faranin shot a look at me. "He needs rest."

"He'd want to help."

"Perhaps tomorrow," Lomen said.

They spent a lot of time discussing how long they should

stick to the defensive plan. I kept pushing for going back to Albuquerque. It was sunset when we all got up from the table, and dusk by the time Len and I finished cleaning up the supper dishes. I tagged along with her back to Madoran's sitting room. Madóran was there, and he'd taken his robe off. Fortunately he had pants on, so I didn't have a heart attack. But I did stand there staring.

He was making a bit of noise opening drawers.

"I cannot find my heavier tunic. I want to wear it for my watch."

"Uh...bathroom?"

Did I mention that ælven guys have gorgeous bodies? All the ones I'd ever seen, anyway.

Madóran turned around and looked at me. I hastily looked at the floor.

"Um, I should go."

"No, wait please."

I heard sliding fabric and looked up. He'd pulled on a tunic, which he usually didn't wear except when gardening.

"You must not take everything Pirian says seriously, Amanda."

"OK," I said.

"He is alben, and while I believe he is not allied with Kanna, he has spent too long feeding on humans to see them as anything but beneath him."

"Yeah, I got that impression."

Never mind that we were beneath all the ælven, too. At least they didn't rub it in. Usually.

He offered to walk me to my room, and I accepted. Even with his company, I kept a nervous eye on the garden as we walked around the *portal*. When we reached my door, Madóran moved to open it.

"Actually, I'd like to visit Savhoran. He can see me home."

"I will go with you."

We continued a couple of steps, then he stopped. "Savhoran needs to feed."

"Yeah, I was telling him that earlier. He said he was going to hunt tonight."

"Ah. I hope he does so."

When we reached Savhoran's door, he knocked. No answer. Madóran frowned, then put his hands and forehead on the door like I'd seen before. After a minute he straightened up and opened the door.

"Savhoran?"

Nothing. Madóran went in and I followed, heart suddenly pounding.

He flipped on a light switch. The room was empty.

= 12 =

Madóran stood frowning at the empty room. He glanced at me, then relaxed his features.

"He must have gone hunting."

"Yeah," I said, but it didn't feel right. My gut was telling me something was wrong.

I thought back to my last conversation with Savhoran. I'd talked about him needing to feed, and he'd agreed. He was upset that I'd talked with Pirian.

"Maybe Pirian heard him leave," I said. The rooms were adjacent.

I felt stupid as soon as I said it. Even if he did hear, what would that tell us? That Savhoran was gone, which we knew.

Pirian was hungry too.

I swallowed. Now that I remembered I was his favorite food, his room was too close to mine for comfort.

Madóran looked at me. "Pirian has pledged to leave my guests alone."

"And you trust him?"

"In this, yes, so long as he is not unduly tempted. Do not approach his room alone."

"Right."

He watched me as I tried to shake off the willies. "You are uncomfortable."

"I'll be all right."

"Would you help me in the great room? The table needs polishing."

"OK."

He was humoring me. It was a kind gesture, though, and

I was grateful.

He gave me rag and a bottle of polish. I was surprised that the bottle was a modern plastic squeeze type, but I figured it was easier to use than a jar. The polish, of course, was homemade. It smelled like beeswax and oranges.

I worked the table over while Madóran walked around the room tidying. I was just about finished when heard an owl outside. I peeked out the nearest window. No owl. Just Madóran, standing out in the driveway past Len's car.

I frowned. Turned around. Saw Madóran by the bookshelf.

I looked back out the window. The figure there moved. It couldn't be Madóran, but it was wearing the tunic he'd been looking for. Right after I told Savhoran that the alben had it in for Madóran.

He moved again, and I was sure. It was Savhoran. My stomach sank so hard I expected to hear a thud.

"No," I whispered.

I ran for the entryway and the front door. No way could I let Savhoran set himself up as bait, not in his weak condition.

"Amanda—"

No time to explain. I opened the door and ran out.

"Amanda!"

I was out and on the driveway. Savhoran wasn't standing where he'd been. I glimpsed him running north across the field.

"Savhoran!"

He didn't hear me. I ran after him, kept yelling. Finally he turned around.

"Amanda! Go back!"

"Not without you!"

I was panting hard. I leaned my elbows on my knees, feeling sick. I still had the bottle of polish in one hand.

Savhoran came running back to me. He caught me by the

shoulders.

Amanda, please go inside.

I know what you're doing, but you can't expect to win when you're starving.

He closed his eyes. *I have to try.*

You have to eat. I'm not going back in unless you come with me or—or feed from me now.

Amanda!

I mean it. You're not going to leave me behind.

I heard a shout from the house and looked back. Madóran was running toward us.

Three things happened really fast.

Savhoran yelled to Madóran in ælven. Madóran tripped and stumbled to his knees.

And the alben female grabbed Savhoran.

I screamed, not in fear as much as in anger. She'd come out of nowhere, and she had Savhoran in a stranglehold, on his knees, in two seconds flat.

~

I did the only thing I could think of. I squirted furniture polish at the alben's face.

Yeah, not a great weapon. It was all I had, and it worked, sort of.

I'd got it in her eyes. She couldn't see, and maybe it stung a little. She sure screamed like it did. She shouted at me too; I figured it was ælven cuss-words.

She still had hold of Savhoran. I was worried she was hurting him. I moved around behind her, slid a foot out and hooked it around her shin, and tugged. Both of them toppled to the ground, but she didn't let go.

I stood over her and squeezed the polish all over her face until the bottle was empty, then dug in my pocket for my pepper spray. She had a mouthful of beeswax and was spluttering. She spat, coughed, and cussed some more.

There was shouting from the direction of the house. The alben heard it too; suddenly she let Savhoran go. She got to her feet, glared at me, and dealt me a roundhouse punch that sent me to the ground.

I was a little woozy for the next few minutes. I'd never been hit like that, not even in playground wars. My ears were ringing and my cheek throbbed.

Someone tenderly hauled me up to a sitting position. My head swam. Arms folded me close, and I knew it was Savhoran. That was his smell, underneath the beeswax.

Voices. I didn't pay attention. Too busy coping.

Savhoran loosened his hold on me and I felt Madóran's hands on my face. Usually they were warm; now they were cool. I sighed as he made the pain ebb away.

Someone carried me into the house. I was too stunned to notice who, but it wasn't Savhoran and I doubt it was Madóran. They took me to my room and laid me on the bed. I heard them talking in ælven. Savhoran said "no" to something; I had a guess what.

I tried to move, but my head didn't like that and my neck was sore. I opened my eyes. Madóran was in the chair by my bed. Savhoran was sitting next to me; I could just see his profile.

Madóran looked at me and touched my face. "You are a brave child."

I shrugged, then winced. "Can't let her beat on my guy."

He laughed. Savhoran leaned over to kiss my forehead.

"She left, huh?" I asked.

"Yes," Madóran said. "Lomen and Bironan were coming from the house. They went after her."

Here we go again.

I didn't want to think about it. Despite Madóran's healing, I felt unwell. I closed my eyes. Savhoran took my hand and squeezed it.

Madóran said something in ælven. Savhoran replied.

"Shall I leave?" I said. Too sarcastic, but I was getting cranky.

"I apologize for my rudeness," Madóran said. "I was telling Savhoran that he must feed tonight."

"I cannot endanger my friends," Savhoran said.

"To accept a small gift will not endanger anyone."

"And another, and another?"

"This situation is unusual."

I kind of thought that everything about the ælven was unusual, but I kept it to myself. If they picked up on my thought, they were polite enough not to show it.

I put some white light around myself. Better late than never.

The next minute I felt a strange prickling on my arms. Opened my eyes and saw them both staring at the east wall of my room. In that direction were the bathroom and the treatment room.

"Your hunger excites his," Madóran said. "Please, Savhoran, for the sake of harmony."

Savhoran didn't say anything. I watched him, wishing I could hold him. Instead I squeezed his hand. Best I could do.

"I know," I said. "I can drive Savhoran to Las Vegas in Len's car. Big enough town, right?"

"You are in no condition to drive," Madóran said.

"Let me nap for an hour or so. Be good as new." I knew that wasn't true, but I did think I'd be able to manage walking and driving in an hour.

"No, that would—"

"I would prefer that," Savhoran said. "At least I will be away from this village."

"Better to let us help," Madóran said.

"No. Even if all of you shared the burden, in the long run

there are not enough of you to aid me without endangering yourselves. I must do this myself. If I knew how to drive, I would go alone."

"Well, you won't let me help the obvious way," I said.

He kissed both my hands. It sent a tingle all through me.

"You are the last person from whom I want such help."

I smiled a little.

"Len or Caeran could drive you," Madóran said.

Savhoran thought about that. I bit my lip. I wanted to be with him, to make sure he didn't do anything suicidal again, but he probably didn't want me around while he went hunting.

"No," Savhoran said quietly. "Amanda made the offer. I would rather go with her."

You could have knocked me over with a feather. If I hadn't already been knocked over.

"Very well." Madóran stood and went to the door. "I will return in two hours to check on you."

When he was gone, Savhoran kissed me: sweetly, tenderly. From the look of pity on his face, I figured I looked pretty awful.

He must have held me until I went to sleep. I woke up alone, in the dark. For a second I panicked, then I felt him — not physically, but through khi I guess. He was sitting in the bedside chair, which he had placed with its back to the door.

"My guardian angel," I mumbled.

"How do you feel?"

I paused to think about it. I had a headache, and the left side of my face ached a little. Probably had a huge bruise, but overall I didn't feel too bad.

Very carefully, I sat up. My head didn't swim. "I'm OK. An aspirin would help."

He didn't say anything, which probably meant he didn't know what aspirin was. Ælven probably never needed it.

"I'm going to turn on the light," I said, reaching for the nightstand.

"All right."

I switched on the bedside lamp, then got up and rummaged in my dresser drawer for aspirin. Found the bottle, and took two with the glass of water Madóran had left for me. Then I risked a glance at the mirror over the dresser.

The light wasn't very bright, but I'd expected to be able to see the bruise. I walked closer to the mirror and turned my head. Only the faintest dark spot right over my cheekbone. I touched it and it felt tender, but didn't scream with pain.

"Damn, he's good."

"Who?"

"Madóran. Look, you can hardly tell."

I went over to Savhoran and he stood up. I showed him my face. He looked sad, then he kissed me gently right on the bruise.

"I am sorry you were hurt."

"Same to you. Did Madóran give you a zap?"

He laughed. "No. She did not hurt me, not as you were hurt."

"What time is it?"

Rhetorical question: the ælven didn't seem to care much about time. I dug out my cell phone and saw that it was almost ten.

It would take almost two hours to drive to Las Vegas. Part of me wanted to crawl back into bed, but I knew I couldn't do that. If Savhoran didn't feed that night he'd be in a bad way. Even I could see that.

I put my phone in my pocket, then checked that my pepper spray was in the other pocket. Not leaving the house without it again.

"Let's go borrow the car keys."

"Let me change my tunic, then I can return Madóran's to

him."

When Savhoran opened the door, I smelled rain. Out in the garden the flagstones were wet, and the water in the fountain was dancing.

The monsoons had arrived, maybe. Regardless, rain is a blessing in New Mexico. I took it for a good sign.

We went to Savhoran's room for him to change, then around to Len and Caeran's room. They were up. Apparently Madóran had talked to them. I expected Caeran to insist that he drive, but he didn't say anything. Len just handed over the keys.

"Want us to come along?"

I bit my lip. Part of me did, but this was a short errand, and I didn't expect to see the alben again that night. She had never attacked twice in a day.

I also suspected Savhoran didn't want spectators.

"Nah," I said. "Thanks, though. We'll be back soon."

"Be careful," she said. "It's raining."

"I will."

I hugged her. Not sure why, just spur of the moment. "I'll buy you a tank of gas," I said.

"Thanks. It needs it."

Savhoran and I went around to the entryway and out the front door. I paused, looking around as if I could spot the alben. Hah.

Maybe Lomen and Bironan had already caught her. That would be sweet.

She probably wouldn't come to the house again that night. We should be all right.

The back of my neck prickled as I told myself that. I looked at Savhoran, who was scanning the horizon. If the alben was around, he'd notice her first.

We got in the car and I checked the gas. About a third of a tank, which should get us to Las Vegas. I started it up and drove down the long driveway to the road. Didn't dare do much over the limit on the unfamiliar roads in wet weather. I paused at the stop sign in Mora, reading signs to make sure I turned the right way.

Something crashed into my car door.

For a second I thought we'd been in an accident. Then it happened again.

I glanced up, saw the alben through my window. Screamed "No!" as she aimed a punch that took out the glass.

I acted purely on instinct. Wrenched the wheel around and gunned the engine.

My hind brain must have told me to head west, away from Las Vegas. I concentrated on staying on the road while driving as fast as possible.

We hit a straight stretch and I sped up. Prayed no cows were wandering on the road at night.

"You OK?" I said.

"Yes."

"Is she following us?"

"Yes."

I floored it, and kept it floored until we got into some twisty mountain roads and I had to slow down. There were steep drop-offs that made me clutch the steering wheel, probably gorgeous in the daytime but scary as hell at night, in the rain.

My heart was pounding. Every minute I was expecting another attack.

We were somewhere southeast of Taos, in the middle of nowhere in the mountains, when the car coughed and died.

"Shit!"

I looked at the gas gauge Empty.

Took out my cell phone, but there were no bars up there in the middle of the mountains.

"Shit, shit, shit!"

I hit the button for the blinkers, then cried. Useless, and dangerous if she was still after us. After a couple of sobs I pulled myself together.

Rain was coming in the window, drenching me. There was broken safety glass in my lap—little sharp nuggets. I opened the door and more spilled out onto the pavement. I got out of the car and carefully brushed the stuff off my lap, then picked a few nuggets off my car seat. Even in the dark, I could tell that the driver door was seriously crunched.

I got back in, pulled the door shut, and locked it. I know, I know.

Savhoran hadn't moved. Hadn't said anything. I had a sudden fear he'd give up.

"Do we stay in the car or get out?"

"Stay."

"But if she follows us, we're toast."

"There is no shelter nearby. I cannot walk far."

Shit.

I turned in my seat to face him. He looked ghastly, and I knew it wasn't just the light from the dashboard.

"Savhoran, you need blood."

I hadn't used the b-word before. He shook his head and stared at his feet.

"We don't have a choice. You need to be strong if she comes for us. I'm counting on you."

"It would strengthen me, but weaken you."

"She'd swat me like a fly anyway. You're my only hope."

He spoke through gritted teeth. "I would rather die than hurt you."

"Would you rather we both died?"

He didn't say anything. The look on his face was awful.

I realized what I had to do.

I reached down and scooped up a handful of glass nuggets from my footwell. Got a few little cuts just doing that. Then I took a deep breath, and squeezed.

Savhoran gasped. "Amanda! No!"

I dropped the glass. I could feel the wet dripping from my hand.

"Sorry," I said, holding it out toward him.

He gave a strangled sound, then grabbed my hand and started sucking. It didn't scare me or creep me out. What I felt was relief.

Through his khi I could tell just how bad off he'd been. He *needed* this.

I leaned my head against the seat and closed my eyes. Tried to relax, and not think about what we were actually doing.

My thoughts drifted back to the blood donor center, where all this had started. That was the first time I saw the alben. Bitch must have been attracted to the smell of the blood.

After a few minutes—less time than it had taken for me to donate a pint of blood—Savhoran raised his head.

"Enough. We must stanch the bleeding."

I didn't have stanching materials. My clothes were all wet. Savhoran pulled off his tunic and wrapped it around my hand.

"It'll stain!"

"No matter."

He held my bundled hand in both of his. I imagined I could feel a tiny healing tingle. He met my gaze with sad eyes.

"I wish you had not done that."

"I apologize. Afraid I can't take it back."

"Never do that again."

I'd only heard that tone in his voice once before: when he claimed the kill of the alben.

"I promise I won't. Just get us out of this, OK?"

He nodded. "I can travel now. We will be safer away from the car. Can you walk?"

"Sure. Let's get to a high place. Maybe I'll get a signal on the cell."

We got out. I slung my pack over my shoulder and stuffed the car keys in my pocket. I'd have some explaining to do to Len—her car was a mess—but first we had to survive.

Abandoning the car, we hiked up the highest piece of mountain at hand. The rain had lightened, but it was cold and I started to shiver. After a few minutes of climbing I was winded. Savhoran picked me up and started up the slope carrying me as if my weight made no difference to him.

He got us up to the top of our mountain and put me down. I pulled out my cell and tried to find a signal. Had to wander around the mountain top a bit, but I finally pulled up enough bars to make a call.

Len answered on the third ring. "Hi, Man. Any luck?"

"Yeah. All bad."

I explained how we'd encountered the alben, and how I'd veered the wrong way and run us out of gas in the middle of the mountains. Oh, and that the alben was probably after us.

I didn't talk about the damage to the car. Time enough for that later, if we made it back to Guadalupita alive.

"Can you come pick us up? Maybe with a posse from the clan?"

"We'll have to borrow a car."

"We're on a mountain top, north of the road," I said, realizing this might not work. "My phone works up here but not down on the road."

"We'll get there, don't worry. Did Savhoran get a chance to feed?"

"Uh...yeah."

"Caeran wants to talk to him."

I held the phone out to Savhoran. He spoke briefly with Caeran in ælven, then gave it back. Caeran had hung up, so I shoved it in my pocket.

"I guess we wait up here," I said.

Savhoran shook his head. "I told Caeran we would retrace our path on foot. The alben thinks we are in the car. When she finds it, she will begin to search for us, but she is more likely to search beyond it than over the ground we already traveled."

"OK. So we keep the road in sight?"

"When it is safe to do so. How is your hand?"

I unwrapped it. Couldn't see well enough to examine it, but I knew I had several cuts, some kind of deep. They had mostly stopped bleeding.

"Guess you don't want this back," I said, dabbing a little ooze of blood with the tunic.

He took it from my hands and threw it down the mountain, on the east side. "She will follow the blood. It may give us some time."

He started down the mountain. I ran to catch up with him.

"Wait!"

He turned. I grabbed him in a hug.

"I love you, OK?"

He embraced me gently, briefly, then stepped away. I took what I could get.

We scrambled down the mountain and began to backtrack, keeping to woods when we had them, hurrying across any open spaces. It wasn't long before I gave up trying to keep up with Savhoran. Now and then he'd pause and wait for me.

I had to rest more and more often. Finally Savhoran picked me up and carried me for a while. I can't say I didn't like it, but I was worried it would make him tired.

It was *not* downhill all the way but I could tell we were gradually descending. I began to hope that we'd make it out of the mountains and I'd be able to call Len.

We came over a rise and I could just glimpse a valley with a couple of lights down in it. We crossed a meadow a stone's throw from the road, heading for the woods on the far side. Once under the trees I couldn't see the valley any more, but I felt more safe.

Savhoran grunted and dropped me.

Oh, shit!

I tried to curl into a ball but I still bashed my elbow hitting the ground. Hurt like crazy but I didn't have time to freak out.

The alben was coming across the meadow.

Savhoran was on his knees. I touched his shoulder and got a taste of what he was feeling. The alben was doing her nasty evil pain thing on him.

I should have run. Any sane person would have, but I was angry and not really sane at that moment.

I looked around for rocks, tree branches, anything I could throw or swing. She was coming fast. With no weapon, I resorted to sports.

I threw myself at her knees.

She wasn't expecting it; probably focused on Savhoran. She let out a startled yelp and went down. That broke her concentration. Savhoran surged to his feet.

Before she could get up, he was on her. I could feel his fury right through the air. It was fast, and I couldn't see well, but I heard bones cracking.

She let out one shriek. In the silence that followed, my ears rang with the sound of it.

Savhoran stood up. I couldn't see his face.

I looked toward the alben. Not breathing, and her head was at an angle that was...wrong.

I didn't know whether to laugh or cry. Enormous relief, but my gentle Savhoran was a killer. It was heartbreaking.

"We can walk on the road now," he said.

He turned and started down. I followed slowly.

Now that the tension was over, tears streamed down my face. I wiped them away with my uninjured hand. Tried not to sniffle.

I don't know how long we walked. It started to rival my forced hike into the mountains. My leg muscles let me know they were not amused. I was cold and felt battered. I started lagging behind.

We were just coming down into the valley where I'd seen the lights, when a car coming toward us started honking. We stepped back from the shoulder. The car, a pickup that had seen better decades, pulled up next to us and stopped, windshield wipers flapping.

"Manda! Are you all right?" Caeran called.

"Yeah. Fine." I waved my good hand.

Len jumped out of the driver's side and ran around to hug me. Lomen, Faranin, and Bironan piled out of the truck bed and surrounded Savhoran. They pelted him with questions in ælven. He gave mostly one-word answers.

Caeran got out and stood listening. When Faranin said something to him he nodded.

The next second, the rest of the ælven took off back into the mountains with Savhoran in the lead. I bit back a protest. They were going to deal with the alben.

Len made me get into the truck between her and Caeran. "God, you're freezing!" she said, and cranked the heater up.

She insisted that I tell her what had happened. I gave her the short version.

The drive back to Madóran's didn't take as long as I'd expected. Savhoran and I had covered a lot of ground. When I moved my legs, I remembered it. I started wishing our host had a hot tub, like Len had teased him about.

Madóran stood waiting for us on the front *portal*. He took one look at me, said something to Caeran, then picked me up and carried me into the house. Caeran opened doors while Madóran carried me to my room.

"I cannot take you to the treatment room," Madóran said. "Pirian is still there."

I didn't want to think about Pirian. Right now, the idea of an alben under the same roof as me was too much. I clung to Madóran until he set me down on my own bed. He lit a fire and then came to examine me.

He looked at my hand, sent Len for some water and bandages, then knelt in front of me. To my surprise he didn't work on my hand, but put his hands on my knees instead. The heat seeped down into my calves like melted butter. I think I let out a moan.

By the time Len came back, my legs felt great. Madóran gently washed the cuts on my hand, bandaged it with gauze, then held it between both of his hands. The pain faded. I sighed with relief.

Len took away the water bowl and stuff. Caeran stayed in the room.

"They're coming back, right?" I asked him.

He nodded. "We burn our dead. It must be done so as not to endanger the forest. They will return when they have finished."

I thought of a pyre deep in the woods, with no mourners. It was decent of them to give her the honor of what I guessed was a proper ælven funeral. More than I would have done.

"I really need a shower," I said, trying to distract myself. I lifted my bandaged hand. "I suppose I shouldn't get this wet?"

"If you do, I will bandage it again. Your comfort is more important."

I took a long, hot shower with my injured hand resting on top of the shower head. Dressed in clean clothes, I felt a lot better. I was dog tired but too wired to go to sleep, and I wanted company. I went to the kitchen.

Everybody was there. Madóran was making hot cocoa. Len and Caeran were sitting at the table eating zucchini bread. Comfort food.

I fetched a glass from the cupboard, filled it with water, chugged, and filled it again. Madóran served the cocoa and we all sat at the table.

"Amanda, will you tell us what happened?"

I swallowed a mouthful. Again, I told the short, non-blood-drinking version. Madóran asked a couple of questions. He looked sad when I described Kanna's death.

"She was a troubled soul," he said. "May she find peace in the spirit realm."

"I guess we can go home now," Len said, putting down her mug, "When should we leave?"

"Perhaps tomorrow," Caeran said, "but I would like to speak with the others before we go."

"No hurry."

I sat trying to relax my hands, which were clenched around my mug. I didn't want to leave without talking to Savhoran.

No, I didn't want to leave *unless Savhoran came too.*

I was a guest. Madóran had housed and fed me for weeks. I had no right to demand more, and now that the problem was resolved, no excuse to stay.

"Hey." Len touched my arm. "You OK?"

I half shrugged, half nodded. I drank the last of my cocoa.

Len grabbed my hand. "Come on."

She dragged me out to the *portal* and went to the nearest door in the glass wall. While she worked the latch open I finally realized we were free.

We went out into the moonlit garden. The moon was waning and had just risen, casting shadows westward. The fountain sparkled in its pale light.

I took a deep breath. The garden was peaceful. A haven. No crazed alben jumping down from the roof.

I heard a door open and looked up. Pirian had come out.

My heart skipped. I nudged Len. We both watched him, ready to run.

He was moving slowly. Come to think of it, I hadn't seen him on his feet since the cave. A dim recollection of my gratitude made me decide maybe he wasn't looking for a late-night snack.

"You need not fear," Pirian said. "I have given my word to Madóran not to harm you. Either of you."

He sat in one of the garden chairs and let out a sigh. Len and I exchanged a glance, then strolled a little closer.

"Are you feeling better?" Len asked.

"I am no longer in pain," Pirian said, "but I am still rather weak."

Len sat in another chair a few feet away from him. I danced back and forth for a second, then gave in and pulled up a third chair. As I dragged it over to them, I noticed Caeran watching from the *portal*. I immediately felt better.

I sat and looked at Pirian. He had his back to the moon—on purpose?—so I couldn't see his face well. He sure did look convalescent, but at least he didn't radiate hunger like he had before.

"Madóran told us about Clan Ebonwatch," I said.

Pirian waved a hand. "They are long gone."

"He thinks there could be a new clan like that. Keeping the..."

Not faith. I looked to Len for help.

"The creed."

Pirian scoffed. "Yes, Madóran clings to his creed."

I glanced at Caeran. "The others—"

"There are any number of fools who follow that painful path. You will not find me among them. I have pain enough."

Discouraging. I was afraid it wouldn't take much to make Savhoran agree with him.

"It would be less lonely," Len said.

"If I were lonely, I would have sought Kanna's company. We have a common loss."

"You loved Gehmanin," I blurted.

Pirian turned his head to stare at me. "Many loved him. He loved only himself, for the most part."

The bitterness in his voice made me regret what I'd said. Not because it wasn't true, mind.

"I suppose Madóran tried to convince him that Ebonwatch could rise again," Pirian added.

Len shrugged. "Gehmanin wouldn't listen. If he had..."

Yeah. Knowing what I knew about Gehmanin, I was glad he hadn't listened.

I felt a little sorry for Pirian, though. He came here looking for someone he loved, and learned that person had been killed. At least his reaction wasn't as extreme as Kanna's.

"Has Madóran told you about the research?" I asked.

Len sat up straight, looked at me, and gave her head a slight shake.

"We have not discussed much," Pirian said.

I ignored Len. "Because he's working on a cure for the curse."

"There is no cure."

"Not yet. Give it a few years."

Pirian slowly turned his head toward Len. "I see. So that is why he tolerates you."

"Tolerate is the wrong word," Madóran said from behind

me.

I turned in my chair to look at him. He had a cup of cocoa in his hand. To my surprise, he gave it to Pirian.

"I have learned there is much merit in humans," he said. "I welcome their friendship."

Pirian sniffed the chocolate, then took a sip. He shook his head. "They live too briefly. Why invest your feelings in them?"

"As a people, they have accomplished much. Perhaps more than we." Madóran gestured toward the cup. "They discovered chocolate. They harnessed electricity. They created machines that fly."

"Useful, I admit. I imagine I will be making use of one shortly."

"You're leaving?" I said, trying to keep from sounding hopeful.

"I have no reason to stay." Pirian took a deep pull on his cocoa. "And since I have promised not to feed on Madóran's guests, I must find sustenance elsewhere."

"You would be welcome to settle here, if you will keep to that pledge," Madóran said.

I gaped at him. Let an *alben* stay in Guadalupita?

"I have plenty of land," Madóran continued. "Caeran's kin are building a house. You could do the same."

"Ah—these would be the couple who left shortly after I arrived?" Pirian said. "Are you sure they would not mind?"

I was sure they would, but it was none of my business.

"I think they would see reason, so long as you agreed not to hunt within, say, twenty leagues," Madóran said.

Pirian chuckled. "So what I heard is true. You are an incurable optimist."

Madóran's face froze for a second. "That is why I came here."

I didn't understand. Looked at Len. She shrugged.

"Thank you for your kind offer," Pirian said, "but I think I must decline. I will refrain from hunting near here, as thanks for your hospitality, for the healing—oh, and for preventing your friends from killing me. They wanted to, yes?"

Madóran didn't answer.

"Yes. Well, I cannot blame them, after Kanna's behavior. I would offer to speak to her again, but I doubt she would listen."

"She's dead," I said.

He looked up at me in surprise. "Dead?"

I nodded. My throat tightened.

"Poor Kanna. I knew this would not end well for her. I did not expect her to die."

"It was her or us."

Ay, yi, yi. I bit my cheek, hoping to keep from saying anything else stupid.

Pirian's eyes turned cold. "No doubt. And where is your beau, my dear?"

"They have all gone to attend to the pyre," Madóran said.

"So it happened tonight." Pirian gazed at me, and my skin crawled. When he spoke again, his voice was deadly soft. "You are fortunate to have powerful friends, little one."

I was about to say I didn't kill her, but then I'd helped, and I sure wasn't sorry. Conflicting emotions kept me from thinking of a clever comeback.

"We should get some rest," Len said, getting up.

She came over and took me by the arm. I let her lead me away. Madóran stayed.

Caeran met us on the *portal* and we walked to their room. They must have done some silent talking, because Caeran went to the south door of the room.

"I will be in the study. Sleep well."

Despite the chocolate, my eyelids were drooping. I didn't

bother with polite protest when Len said I'd share her bed. I let her put me in a nightshirt and crawled under the covers, grateful not to be alone.

= 13 =

I had bad dreams. Poor Len had to wake me up a few times. She probably didn't get much sleep.

By morning I was even more exhausted. My hand was throbbing, and I was sure that Savhoran must hate me. He'd hated me a lot in my dreams, which involved me clumsily cutting myself again and again.

But I knew that the real problem was that I'd done it deliberately.

I lay in bed for a long while, feeling sorry for myself. Gradually I realized Len was gone. I raised my head and saw sunlight around the edges of the curtains.

I dragged my ass out of bed and put on my clothes. Folded the nightshirt and left it on the dresser. Stood wondering what to do.

Breakfast? My stomach rebelled at the idea. I knew what I had to do.

I opened the door and looked out at the *portal*, still not used to the idea that I could walk out there safely. I went around and stopped at Savhoran's door. Knocked, then leaned my head against the wood.

It's me. Can I come in?

Maybe they weren't back yet. Maybe he wasn't coming back.

I squeezed my eyes shut, fighting tears. *Please let me in.*

No answer. Not that I could really tell, but it felt like he wasn't there.

I went to my own room and lay on my bed and cried. Woke to a knock at the door.

"Gway," I said into my pillow.

"It's lunchtime," Len said through the door. "You missed breakfast."

"Not hungry."

"Madóran thought you'd say that. I've got a tray for you."

Shit.

I sat up and blew my stuffy nose. Len assumed this was an invitation and tried the knob, but it was locked. I didn't remember doing that.

I went to let her in. The tray was a bowl of green chile stew, a fresh tortilla, and a side of zucchini bread, with a glass of milk to tame the chile. I should have been hungry, but I couldn't face the food. I accepted the tray and put it on the dresser. Len followed me in, so I took a piece of zucchini bread and nibbled a corner. Tasted like sawdust.

We both sat on the bed. I struggled not to cry. My eyes were sore already.

Len put her arm around me.

"He didn't come back," I said in a choked voice.

"Yes, he did. We were asleep. Madóran said they had a long talk. Savhoran's gone up to the spring."

"Spring?"

"There's a hot spring up in the hills. It's on Madóran's property."

"Savhoran's up there? It's daytime!"

"There's a cave nearby. He's doing a cleanse. It's kind of like a sweat lodge."

A cleanse. Trying to forget.

I hadn't told anyone about what I'd done with the safety glass, but Madóran had probably guessed. Or maybe Savhoran had told him.

My eyes started leaking. I wiped at my face, but it was no good.

Len handed me a tissue. "He'll be OK."

"I think I really screwed up."

Len did what a good friend does. She held me and let me cry. She stopped trying to tell me it was all right. She passed me the box of tissue when I couldn't breathe anymore.

I mopped my face. Len handed me the water glass from my nightstand. I took a deep gulp.

"Did he tell you?" I said.

"Who? What?"

I swallowed. "Did Madóran tell you what happened last night?"

"You told me."

"I didn't tell you everything." I drained the glass and handed it back. "The car was dead, and Savhoran was too tired to walk. We were sitting ducks. So I picked up a handful of glass and made myself bleed."

"Oh."

"And now he hates me."

"Maybe not."

"Yeah, because he didn't want to. I made him do it."

"Sounds like there wasn't much choice," Len said.

"There wasn't. She'd have had us. But it was still against his will."

"Wait until he comes back. You guys need to talk."

"What if he doesn't?"

"He will, honey. He will."

She rubbed between my shoulder blades, which made me realize how tense my back was. I closed my eyes and soon she had me prone on the bed, massaging my back like a pro. She knew right where it was sore.

I wanted to ask Len to take me to the spring, but I knew it was a bad idea. I'd already been too pushy with Savhoran.

I composed apologies in my head. They all sounded lame.

By the time Len stopped rubbing, I was a puddle. She nudged me to sit up and blackmailed me into eating some of the food. Said she wouldn't leave until I'd taken five bites of chile and two each of tortilla and zucchini bread.

"That's nine," I said. "Why nine?"

"Because I said so. Eat."

I ate. Then I let her nag me into going out into the garden. I sat in the shade and watched the birds play in the fountain. Beautiful, but I couldn't work up any enthusiasm.

I spent the afternoon there. Len brought me lemonade, which I drank. I dozed a little in the heat.

When Madóran summoned me to dinner I went, not because I was hungry but because it was easier than arguing. The whole clan was there, even Nathrin and Mirali—everyone except Savhoran.

I took some food and nibbled at it. Not really hungry. The wine tasted good though—I drank a glass pretty fast and Madóran refilled it.

Nathrin and Mirali wanted to know about what had happened with Kanna. Caeran did the explaining, for which I was grateful. Then Len asked about the pyre and Lomen answered.

"It took some time to prepare. There was plenty of dead wood, but we had to search for an open space to burn it. We found a dried water-hole and built the pyre there. It burned quickly. We stayed until it was out."

"Thank you," I said, thinking of the bad forest fires we'd had.

Lomen bowed to me. "Thank *you*. We are aware of your contribution."

I felt my cheeks flash hot. Looked down at my plate full of uneaten food.

"I salute you, Amanda Richards," Lomen said. "Clan Greystone is in your debt."

They all raised their glasses. I couldn't help wondering if Savhoran would agree with them.

I should have said thank you, but my throat had closed up. I took a sip of water.

Lomen took pity on me and changed the subject. "Caeran, will you and Len be returning to the city?"

"As long as Len is studying at the university, we will live there."

"Probably longer," Len said. "I'll need access to labs, once I know what the hell I'm doing."

"What you need," I said, "is a foundation."

They all looked at me. I took a breath.

"I've been thinking about your plan. Len wants lab access to do research. I know you have some financial resources—" I glanced at Madóran. "—but you haven't really figured out to apply them. Just getting a lab job won't guarantee you'll have the time and materials to do the work you need. If you start a foundation now, though, you can set it up to get grants and stuff. The labs and schools will take you more seriously."

"I don't know anything about grants," Len said.

"Me neither, but I know how to find out. If I take some classes at the business school I can probably help you."

Len's face filled with joy. "Amanda! Thank you!" She jumped up and hugged me.

"I'm not pledging my life to this, OK? Just offering to help set things up."

"That's fine! That's wonderful, thank you so much!"

"I think Amanda should be made a member of the clan," said Lomen.

There were murmurs of agreement, though Mirali scowled. I didn't care what she thought so much as I cared what Savhoran thought. I cleared my throat.

"Thanks, Lomen, but um. Savhoran might not..."

I couldn't finish. They got the message. Faranin asked Nathrin something about the new house, and they all politely ignored me while I tried not to go to pieces. Tears were stinging my eyes. I got up and left, as quietly as I could.

I went out the near door, heading for the garden. Sunset was painting the tall clouds to the west orange and pink. It hadn't rained, but there was that tension in the air that said it might.

They left me alone, even Len. There wasn't anything more to say. I stayed in the garden until it got dark. Pirian came out, at which point I went to my room. He and I traded polite smiles, that was all.

I lay there feeling miserable, hoping that Savhoran would come back that evening. Rehearsed my apologies some more. Finally I drifted off.

This time I woke up early. I heard birds twittering outside.

Savhoran hadn't come back that night. If he had he'd have knocked on my door. Wouldn't he?

To avoid being rousted out of bed again, I got dressed and went to the kitchen. Madóran was cooking. I offered to help. He sent me to pull some green onions from the garden.

I picked up gloves and hat from the workroom as usual. The minute I stepped outside I froze.

Outside the house. No one to guard me.

I swallowed. Reminded myself that she was dead. I had helped. They'd burned her body and she wasn't coming back.

I walked slowly through the rows of vegetables, watching to either side. Found the onions and stood there, looking all around. It was a pretty morning with white puffy clouds beginning to form, promising a chance of rain later in the day. Why was I nervous?

I pulled a couple of handfuls of onions and hurried back inside. Madóran had me wash them and chop them up for omelets. He was cracking eggs into a bowl.

"Did Savhoran come back last night?" I asked, trying to sound casual.

"No. I went up to the spring to talk to him early this morning."

"Oh. He's OK, right?"

Madóran sighed and turned to me. "Not entirely. He was traumatized, as were you, by the events of the previous night."

I swallowed. "Is he mad at me?"

"I think not, but he is angry with himself for being weak."

"Weak?!"

"Amanda, I know what you did. I think you made the right choice. Savhoran knows this too, in his heart, but he feels he should have been able to resist the temptation you offered him."

I put down the knife. "For Pete's sake, how? He was starving! I did everything but slit my throat."

"He is thinking in terms of the ideal. We are not as practical as your kind, Amanda. We have no time limitations, so we aim for perfection. Having been unable to maintain the state of perfection he hopes for, Savhoran feels he has failed."

I shook my head. I had thought I was beginning to understand the ælven, but apparently not.

"Remember, Savhoran has already had to compromise his ideal. He is still trying to reconcile his illness with his desire to keep the creed."

"And I just made it harder."

"Harder, but not impossible. Be patient. He needs time to think through what has happened and come to terms with it."

I nodded. I should probably do that too. What I wanted was to know that Savhoran would forgive me, but that wasn't going to happen right away.

I wondered how much time he would need to sort it out. A week? A month? He had all the time in the world, but I didn't.

I picked up the knife and carefully finished chopping the onions, then put them in a bowl for Madóran. He beat the eggs to a froth with a whisk, then poured them into one of two cast iron skillets on the stove. He had me grate cheese while he put the kettle on for tea. Then he started a second batch of eggs.

Helping him cook calmed me down. My love life might be a mess, but the world still had butter melting into fresh bread hot from the oven.

Faranin came in and spoke to Madóran in their language. Madóran answered in English, which was nice of him. People started drifting in for breakfast. I got out plates, mugs, silverware, napkins. Kept myself busy so I wouldn't have to talk.

We set up the food as a buffet on the counter. There weren't enough chairs around the table, so Len, Caeran, and I went over to sit on the banco.

"Man, we'd like to go home today if it's OK with you," Len said. "Hard to believe, but it's time to think about registering for the fall semester."

She was right. We'd been here a chunk of the summer.

I swallowed. "OK."

"We'll stay in touch," she added.

I nodded. My stomach had clamped down. I got up and refilled my tea mug. Left my plate on the counter.

We were leaving. I wasn't going to see Savhoran again before we did.

I strolled out onto the *portal* and looked at the garden. I'd miss it, even though I hadn't been able to sit out there as much as I wanted. Maybe because of that.

I'd miss all of it. Grubbing in the garden, Madóran's wonderful meals, the people. Even Mirali, who I was pretty sure didn't like mortals. Even Pirian.

Well, maybe not Pirian.

I finished my tea, took my mug back to the kitchen, and went to my room to pack. It didn't take nearly long enough. I slipped down the *portal* to the room that Savhoran had been using. Opened the door, hoping for a glimpse of something to remember him by.

It was tidy. Bed made, nothing sitting out. The room looked unoccupied.

Disappointed, I carried my bag to the front entryway and set it down near the door. I heard music from the great room, so I went in to listen. Madóran was playing the guitar, fingerstyle, very good.

We'd had a few musical evenings. I wished there'd been more.

I sat on the couch and watched his fingers dance over the strings. He was good at everything. Really made a girl feel inferior.

"There is one thing that humans are better at than we," Madóran said.

"Oh, sorry. Forgot to shield."

"You have children far more easily."

I nodded. "This is the reason for some of our problems."

"Yes, but they are problems we would dearly love to have. Ours are the opposite. And for Savhoran, it is a very big problem."

He finished the piece and put down the guitar. "You see, it is our females who have difficulty conceiving. Human females do not."

I nodded. "Actually, we spend a lot of time trying not to."

"An attitude we cannot fathom. Do you see why this causes Savhoran confusion?"

I frowned. I could see why it confused the ælven in general. Why Savhoran?

"With you, he could easily father a child, something every ælven dreams of."

I did *not* want to have this conversation again.

"We talked about that. I'm not ready to start a family."

"You are very young, even for your kind. Yes, I understand. But, you see, a family with you is likely his only chance. He cannot couple with an ælven female without putting her at risk, and any child of such a union would suffer the curse."

He picked up the guitar again. I sat thinking for a bit, listening to the gentle music. Slowly it dawned on me: the fact that Madóran had mentioned this issue meant that he thought Savhoran had been thinking about it. Had they discussed it?

My gut turned a slow flip. I pulled a notebook out of my pack and started writing a note to Savhoran. Had to start over a few times. Madóran politely ignored the balled-up rejects I tossed on the floor.

I managed to put together an apology that wasn't whiny. I wasn't sorry that Savhoran had killed the alben, but I was sorry I'd forced him to feed on me. I was positive there wasn't any other choice. I didn't say that in the note; he knew. I didn't make any excuses or try to justify what I'd done. I just apologized.

I carefully tore out the page and folded it. Wrote Savhoran's name on the outside. Held it for a minute, then put it on the coffee table by Madóran.

"Would you give that to him when he comes back?" If he comes back. I pushed that thought away.

"Of course," Madóran said. "And I am fairly certain that he will."

I heard a door open, and Len and Caeran came in from

the entryway. This was it. I stood up.

Madóran put down the guitar and stood too. Len came over and gave him a big hug. He said something ælven to her, and she nodded.

I'd barely started to learn ælven. Maybe now I never would.

Madóran came to me, offering a hug. I took it. Needed all the hugs I could get.

"Thanks for letting me stay," I said.

"You are always welcome here, Amanda. Len and Caeran are here often. I hope you will come with them sometimes."

"I'd like that."

He picked up a book from the table and offered it to me. It was the ælven book we'd been using.

"To help you with your studies."

"But this is your only copy!"

"Perhaps you can make a copy for yourself. It would be good practice."

I held the book to my chest. "I'll take good care of it. Thank you."

We shuffled outside. Instead of Len's car, a dark green Camry sat out front.

"That's right." I looked at Len. "Your car. Was it totaled?"

"Close enough. We had it towed to a junkyard that wanted it for parts. Caeran and I went down to Las Vegas yesterday and found this at a used car place."

Bigger and nicer than the Subaru. The upholstery was clean, the back seat was deep and wide, and it didn't smell funny.

Caeran must have bought it. How rich was he, anyway? He had like three changes of clothes that I knew of.

We said a last goodbye to Madóran and drove off. I stared out the back window until I couldn't see the hacienda anymore. Madóran stood there watching the whole time.

I thought over the text of my apology again and again. Would it piss Savhoran off? Had it been a mistake? Too late now.

I fell into a funk, thinking about him. A couple of times Len said something to me and I had to ask her to repeat it. Finally I closed my eyes so they'd think I was asleep.

We got into Albuquerque late afternoon. Thunderheads were building over the city. Good chance of rain.

I went into my room and sat on the bed, feeling out of place. Staying with Len and Caeran had been fine for the summer, but indefinitely? This was their house. I didn't really belong.

Back to the dorm, them. Woohoo.

College seemed so far away from what we'd been doing over the last couple of months. Contemplating classes felt bizarre.

The next day, we went to the campus to get registered. Caeran came too; he was going to take classes this year. Len wanted his support on the research project. I spent a long time looking at the courses at the school of business, and picked out three that I thought would help me figure out how to set up a foundation for the ælven.

We got all our school stuff together: textbooks, notebooks, etc. That took another day, then I had nothing left to do but mope. Two more weeks until classes started.

I dialed Savhoran's cell. It rang in the house: they'd never got it back to him. Caeran shut it off and looked at me.

"Savhoran's apartment should be secured. Will you help?"

"OK."

I hadn't been in the apartment before, so I was curious. All three of us went.

There were no decorations of any kind, no personal things. Heavy blinds over all the windows. Some very utilitarian furniture and some pans and dishes in the kitchen that looked brand new. Savhoran hadn't invested anything of himself in this place. The most personal item we found was his cell phone charger.

He hadn't intended to stay. Or he hadn't decided.

"Jeez, this is awful," Len said to me. "What do you say we fix it up?"

I shrugged. "OK."

We went to the home store and bought paint, wastebaskets, and a few nicknacks. Len had me pick them out, and without my realizing it a theme emerged. I chose sage green paint, curtains with leaves all over them, a graceful flower-shaped candle holder, and a small statue of a squirrel. Without any deliberate intention, I was making a forest scene.

All I was thinking was: what would Savhoran like? Maybe he would like it, if he ever saw it.

Len and I spent the next couple of days painting. Boring, laborious work but it made me feel better. When we were done the place looked a lot nicer, even without furniture.

We fixed that with a trip to a bedding store. Got a nice foresty comforter set, pale green sheets, curtains, and a comfy futon chair for the living room, big enough for two if they were friendly.

"There ought to be a TV," Len said, standing by the chair and looking at the blank wall opposite.

"I don't think Savhoran watches TV," I said.

"So? You do."

"It's not my place."

Len sat on the futon chair. "Actually, Caeran and I have been talking. He paid a year's rent in advance on this place. No sense in it sitting empty. We love having you, but I've been getting the feeling you need more space. Why don't you stay here until Savhoran comes back?"

"He's not coming back." I swallowed. Hadn't said that out loud before.

"I don't know. He's still at Madóran's."

I looked at her. I wanted to hope, even though it hurt.

Len smiled. "He's working things out, that's all. The ælven always take a long time to think about things."

I looked around at the apartment. It still smelled like paint, but it looked pretty good. I'd been trying to make a nice home for Savhoran. I couldn't help making it a place that I liked too.

Two days later I moved in.

I still spent a couple of hours over at Len and Caeran's every day, studying the ælven book and working on making a copy by hand. Didn't dare take that precious book to a copy machine, and I didn't feel right taking it out of the house. My copy wouldn't be beautiful, but I'd be able to use it.

Len insisted that I have dinner with them every night. I didn't argue much on that one—Caeran was a pretty good cook.

With afternoons and evenings taken care of, I was only in the apartment nights and mornings. That was still plenty of time to be lonely.

I cried a lot. Thought about Savhoran. Wondered what it would be like to try to just have a normal human life, now that I'd been exposed to the ælven. I suspected it was impossible.

Savhoran was all I wanted. I couldn't imagine dating a human guy after this. Maybe I'd just had bad luck, but most of the guys I had dated were total drips.

I would help Len and Madóran with the science project, since I didn't have much else to do. Other than that, I was pretty much on hold.

Days went by, becoming weeks. Classes started. I did all right in the business classes, and even got curious about the stuff I was learning. It was organized and made sense, a comforting contrast to my life for the past few months.

Evenings we'd all study together at Len and Caeran's. One night after banging my head against an assignment, I went back to the apartment, put my key in the lock, and and stopped.

It was already unlocked.

A tingle of fear went down my spine. I took a step back from the door. Run first or call 911?

The door opened and Savhoran looked out.

I squeaked and threw myself at him. Not the best idea, but it was spontaneous.

He put his hands on my waist and gently pushed me away. His eyes were still haunted with sadness.

I tried to pull myself together. "It's so wonderful to see you!"

That got a faint smile out of him. "I am glad to see you, also. I have come to offer you my atonement."

"Atonement? Why?"

"For what I took from you."

I took a deep breath. "That was a gift. You don't owe me anything. Hell, I'm the one that owes you!"

"Please, Amanda. Let me do this."

He looked weary. I bit my lip and shut up.

Savhoran took something out of the pouch on his belt and put it in my hand, then wrapped both his hands around it. He spoke in ælven, not to me but sort of over my head. I didn't understand most of it, but I caught "thanks" and "may the spirits."

He let go of my hand and stepped back. I looked at his gift: a tiny deer no longer than my pinkie, perfectly carved out of bone.

"It's beautiful. Madóran's been teaching you."

"I have carved for centuries."

I looked up at him and swallowed. "Thank you."

"You owe me no thanks."

"Just let me be grateful, OK? Because I can't help it. I'm grateful to know you."

To my alarm, tears started leaking out of my eyes. I turned away and headed for the bedroom.

"I've been crashing here. I'll get my stuff out of your way."

I carefully set the carved deer on top of the brand-new dresser, then took out my bag, dumped it on the bed, and opened the top dresser drawer. I wiped at my face and tried not to sniffle.

"No need," Savhoran said, coming to the doorway. "I do not mean to stay."

Ouch. I took a shaky breath.

"It's your place."

"It is Caeran's place. You have more need of it than I."

"But we fixed it up for *you*."

I sat on the bed and buried my face in my hands. Stupid, stupid! No better way to drive a guy away then to whine and cry. I struggled to stop.

"Amanda."

He stroked my hair. I dissolved into sobs. He sat beside me and put his arms around me and let me cry.

I should have been deliriously happy to see him again. It was just that he'd confirmed my worst fear—he planned to leave. He didn't want to be with me.

"The apartment is beautiful," he said. "You have made it a home."

I sniffed and mopped my face. "For you."

"I will camp by the river."

I gulped. "Here in town? In the *bosque*?"

"*Bosque*. Yes."

That was actually good news. He wasn't moving back to

Europe, or anywhere else inaccessible.

"Guess you'd rather live outdoors than in an apartment," I said. "I can understand."

"It is not because of preference. I have spent many evenings talking with Madóran and with Pirian."

"Pirian! He's still there?"

"Not now. He and I left together."

"You mean he's here in Albuquerque?"

"Yes. He means to patrol the mountains, while I patrol the river."

I blinked at Savhoran. He still had his arm around me, and he was gazing into the distance.

"We have decided to follow Ebonwatch's path, if we can. We will atone for our hunting as Ebonwatch did, and watch over humankind in the place where we live. If we succeed in living by the creed, we can recruit others who share our misfortune. Someday we may have a clan."

"*Pirian* agreed to that?"

"I believe he thinks we will fail, but at least he was intrigued enough by the idea that he is willing to try. He is not unreasonable, merely accustomed to his habits."

I swallowed. Habits like thinking humans weren't worth the bother of getting emotionally involved. Would Savhoran someday be accustomed to that idea too?

"He has promised me that he will leave you and Len alone," Savhoran said.

"I thought he already promised that."

"No, he had promised to leave Madóran's guests alone. You are no longer his guests."

Crap. Freaking literal-minded ælven. Lucky I hadn't run into Pirian on campus.

"He will not harm you. He knows that if he did, I would slay him as an oath-breaker."

Savhoran gave my shoulders a squeeze, then let go and

turned to face me. "My hope is that you will never be hurt again, by me or others of my kind."

I frowned. "You want me not to be hurt."

"Yes."

"Then don't leave. Stay with me. Let me l-love you."

I could have kicked myself. Nothing that corny had ever left my mouth before.

Savhoran took a deep breath. "If I stay, you will surely be hurt. You are mortal, and I am not."

"Don't you dare make that excuse! I don't care if you still look twenty when I'm a gray-haired granny. People will just think I'm a cradle-robber."

Savhoran's face got grim. "That is another reason I should not stay. You will want children someday. I cannot..."

He looked down and swallowed. I grabbed his hands.

"I don't care. We can adopt. That's not a problem, just don't leave."

I kissed his cheeks a dozen times. Finally he raised his head.

"Amanda—"

"I have faith in you. You'll succeed. You'll live by the creed and gather a big clan and you'll all help each other. But that clan will need a human mascot, right? Caeran's clan has Len. You can have me."

He closed his eyes, and I was afraid I'd offended him. Then he laughed.

It was like the sun rising. OK, not a good analogy for Savhoran, but that's how it made me feel. Hope.

"You will not let me refuse, will you?"

I smoothed his hair back. "Nope."

He leaned into my hand, and a slow burn started in my gut. All my worries vanished. I put my arms around him and kissed him.

I knew he'd been holding back, but I didn't know how

much. He kissed me like I'd never been kissed, and the rest of the world went away for a while.

All I can say is wow. I was definitely spoiled for human guys.

He paused to let me catch my breath. "I have one request," he said.

"Hm?"

"Do not donate blood again."

I thought about the blood center. They were always begging for more donors, but they'd have to do without me. I didn't think I'd be able to go back in there anyway.

"You got it," I said.

Thank you, Amanda.

I caught my breath. I hadn't felt him like that in a while. If I could feel like that every day, even just for a minute, it would be worth any pain that might come my way.

About the Author

Pati Nagle was born and raised in the mountains of northern New Mexico. An avid student of music, history, and humans in general, she loves the outdoors but hides from the sun.

She writes in a variety of genres, but is most often drawn to fantasy or (as P.G. Nagle) historical fiction. Her stories have appeared in *Asimov's Science Fiction*, the *Magazine of Fantasy & Science Fiction*, and in various other magazines and anthologies, including *Elf Magic*, which featured "Kind Hunter," the story that sparked the ælven world. Her Blood of the Kindred series includes *The Betrayal*, *Heart of the Exiled*, and *Swords Over Fireshore*. A contemporary series featuring the ælven began with *Immortal* and continues with *Eternal*.

Pati Nagle still lives in the mountains in New Mexico with her husband and lots of wildlife. She loves to walk in the woods and look up at the stars.

Pati Nagle's websites:

www.patinagle.com
www.pgnagle.com

Other Books by Pati Nagle

Immortal Series

Immortal
Eternal

Blood of the Kindred Series

*Before the human race evolved, the ælven were locked in a war with their
kindred and foes, the blood-drinking alben*

The Betrayal
Heart of the Exiled
and
Swords Over Fireshore

read samples at aelven.com

www.ingramcontent.com/pod-product-compliance
Lightning Source LLC
Chambersburg PA
CBHW020404120726
47904CB00002B/701